MATCH

MATCH

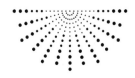

EMMA GRACE

THE PAPER HOUSE
PUBLISHING

CONTENTS

For my sister Rebecca,
my very own Lucas.

FOUR YEARS AGO...

Warped plywood groaned under my weight as I knelt in the pitch-black attic. Ava, Noah, and Chris hoisted themselves through the opening behind me, causing the treacherous floor to let out a loud creak. As I moved, my stomach cramped in pain; I winced, trying to keep still. The doctors said I wouldn't feel this way again after tomorrow's surgery, but I just couldn't wait to get up here.

"Your family sleeps well, right?" Chris asked, doubt seeping into his voice.

I barely paid attention as I shined my flashlight around the narrow space. "Yeah."

The ceiling was about six feet high at its peak, which meant that Ava and I were the only ones who could stand up straight. We were looking for a duct-taped cardboard box with the words *Nana Sophia's* scrawled across the top. My father first put it up when the new floor was put down. It had been nine long years since then, but things in the attic had a tendency to sit untouched forever.

Ava grimaced when her hands touched the damp plywood. "Ugh, gross."

I hushed her and crawled to the corner where I knew the box was, holding the flashlight between my teeth and trying not to touch the exposed insulation.

"Got it," I said, pulling it to the center of the floor so we could all see. The writing on the front of the box was smeared with water stains, and the duct tape was peeling off at the edges.

"Why is this so important, again?" Chris asked, shivering against the damp cold.

"Nana Sophia was my great-something-grandmother," I explained, using a kitchen knife to saw away at the cardboard. "She was in the first Matching Ceremony and kept a diary through it."

"Awesome," Noah said, standing half-hunched in the middle of the room.

"It separated her and her fiancé," I replied.

"Less awesome."

"Yep." The slimy cardboard fell apart in my hands and spilled its guts to us. Inside was an old leather diary, a few framed photographs, and a crescent moon necklace.

"You guys ready?" I asked, looking back up at them.

"Duh." Noah grinned.

"Sure." Chris was smiling, too.

Ava waved her hands, which was her way of telling me to hurry up.

Just like I predicted, they all seemed excited about the prospect of learning about the world as it really was before the Matching. What little history we learned in school had been contradictory, blatant lies. We had never learned any details, probably because the adults didn't know how much to tell us, or they didn't even know themselves.

We sat in the middle of my old, slimy attic with our four flashlights locked in on the scrawling cursive. Our eight eyes ate every word, and our four hearts pounded out of our four chests.

There's finally going to be a wall! Thank Ankou, we finally get a wall built around our little town to keep us safe. There have been so many attacks recently—people driving trucks straight into crowds, bombs planted every-where. The world is a mess. We'll be safe here; the wall will finally protect us.

The new hospital is being built down the road, and the grocery store was expanded so that we can stay here without ever having to leave. It's the perfect way to live. All that we need will be right here, and none of us will have to risk getting hurt again. Poor Mrs. Fletcher almost got assaulted last week while running to an appointment in Pevidere. The world is in shambles these days.

That was only the first entry. Chris, Ava, Noah, and I stared at each other in wonder.

Ava sat back on her heels. "This... this is real."

"So they *wanted* a Border?" Noah asked.

"I guess so," I replied. It was nearly impossible to believe someone could've wanted to be trapped when the four of us only wanted to get out. Maybe the outside world wasn't as great as we all thought, but it had been decades since she wrote this diary. Maybe things had changed.

"This is some crazy shit we just stuck our feet in," Chris muttered. His eyes pierced me in the dark, two blue beacons in a pale field of pimples.

Having the diary was illegal, reading it was illegal, and being out of your family's home after curfew was illegal. We could've all been arrested, but it was worth it. My father had told me about this diary two days prior, how it had the secrets of life before the Border. He said I was old enough to know but not to tell anyone outside of our immediate family.

I had told Ava over lunch the next day, too excited to keep it to myself. She told Noah, who told Chris, who told me the three of them were going to sneak over in the middle of the night to investigate with me. They simply climbed the oak outside my window on this moonless night and shimmied inside, but they scared me half to death when I woke to the three of them standing over my bed.

Chris shined a flashlight on his watch. "Guys, why don't we all go home for the night? It's four a.m., and we have that big exam tomorrow." He looked at me to gauge my reaction, being the only one I even told about tomorrow's surgery. I had decided to fake sick the next day, so Ava and Noah didn't worry, although knowing Noah, he would anyways.

The next day was our grade-passing exam. We needed it to move up to the next level, but there were multiple days we could take it. We'd all opted for the next day so that we could take it together, but I would have to wait a few days. As long as I took it before the communal birthdate, it was fine.

Everyone in Carcera, our community, shared a birthdate: January 1st. When we were infants, we weren't allowed to go home with our parents until that day, regardless of when we were born. Our parents came for daily visits but couldn't take us home or give us toys or clothes because we were born to serve the government. The lack of interaction with our parents was our earliest conditioning to put service to the country first and family second. Even so, my family had a small, semi-secret communal birthdate party for ourselves; we exchanged gifts, and my mother would make a small cake or, if we were lucky, one of her famous pecan pies.

Despite that small act of rebellion, my parents refused to tell me my real birthdate even though I begged them to. I wanted to know when my lungs began to breathe, and my eyes began to see. I wanted to know the exact moment I was born into this cage so that, despite the iron bars around my life, I could still do my best to celebrate it.

CHAPTER ONE

MY BROTHER LUCAS is shouting at me from downstairs. "Katie, let's go!"

"Give me *one* second!" I jam what must be the 50th bobby pin into my hair. Usually, it's a nice thing to have soft hair, but not today. Elegant buns are nearly impossible, with hair as feathery and thin as mine.

"We have to leave!" he shouts, footsteps rushing up the stairs. He barges into my room in a flurry of too-long arms and legs.

"Knock, you jerk!" I laugh, moving over to look in the mirror. My laughter is just a cover-up of how nervous I am.

Tonight is our seventeenth birthdate and Matching Ceremony. We will go to the Hall and become Matched with our soulmates. We will marry these soulmates, have two children with them, and die by their sides many years from now. A piece of paper will determine the course of my entire life in less than three hours; I have not eaten all day.

"We have to *go*." Lucas nearly whines. "It's nine-thirty already."

I shove the 51st bobby pin into my bun and unleash hairspray upon it. "Lucas, the Matching Ceremony starts at eleven."

"Yeah, but the bus is always so crowded when it gets late," Lucas argues. He always likes to be early; somehow, I am always late.

"But then we just have to sit there and be bored," I retort. My shimmering, dark blue dress clings to my legs, making me feel claustrophobic.

My room is the size of everyone else's to symbolize that we are all equal. These houses are cookie-cutter, and my belongings are, too. A black desk sits in one corner with a cream-colored lamp and some green and blue notebooks for school. My closet is filled with solid-colored clothes, symbolizing that I am not yet Matched. In one week, I will go to the clothing depot on my own and pick up my first set of multicolored clothes. The rest of the community will finally recognize me as an adult.

Lucas leans against my dresser in defeat, knocking over my hairbrush but ignoring it. At least I'm not as clumsy as he is, although I tend to trip over my feet occasionally. Ava's tried to teach me some ballet, but I'm a horrible dancer.

He sighs. "Fine." His eyes light up after a moment, letting me know he has a mischievous idea. He sighs dramatically, forcing a smile off his face and hanging his head. "I guess today *isn't* the most important day of our lives. I guess today *doesn't* decide our futures. I guess *not*."

He's right—today *is* the most important day of our lives. We've been waiting to know our Matches since we were old enough to grasp the importance of the necklaces. I once tried to see if Chris and I Matched, but we were scolded by our teacher as soon as she saw. I remember how she shrieked, "Matching is a sacred event that should not be spoiled. The crime is punishable with life in jail!" She was probably making the last part up just to scare us, but I haven't tried to find my Match since. Mrs. Gutale was vulture-esque and terrifying.

"Oh, shut up." I toss a bobby pin at him. "Don't make me hairspray you."

"No!" he cries, cowering. "Not the hairspray! Anything but that!"

I spray a puff at him, and he shrieks, plastering himself to the wall to avoid the foul-smelling chemicals.

We both laugh, his being an octave above mine as I continue my assault. His voice used to be much higher than mine, but when we turned 14, he hit a growth spurt. Now he towers over me, and I hate to admit that he's much stronger, too, but his laugh still sounds ridiculous.

"Why do you sound... like that?" I laugh. Only my twin can make me laugh like this.

Our giggles eventually subside, replaced by an uncomfortable silence as we remember how scared we are, and how important today is.

I study his face—there is a dusting of freckles across his nose that I don't have. We both inherited our mother's medium brown hair, which lightens into an almost auburn color in the summer. Our father gave us hazel eyes, although mine are greener than Lucas's. His eyebrows are thicker than mine, but we both have the same stubby eyelashes.

Two years from today, we will be packing our things to move into our government-assigned homes to live with our Matches. We will be preparing to leave this house in exactly two years. Lucas won't sleep in the next room over, and his toothbrush won't sit next to mine in the bathroom cabinet. I won't see him every day. What will my life be like without the constant there-ness of my brother? Did my parents think they would always be with the siblings they never see anymore?

"You ready?" he asks, voice filled with false confidence. I know he's faking it because I am, too.

"You know how I feel, Lucas," I mumble, voice low so our parents don't overhear.

"And you know how I feel," he replies. He's right—I do.

We walk down the unforgiving wooden stairs to meet our parents in the kitchen without another word. He leads, coming to the same hard floor at the bottom. Our stairs sit in the center of our house, with a wall on one side and a railing on the other. Lucas and I used to fly down them in our socks and hook ourselves around the banister, flinging ourselves into a pile of pillows. Our mother told us to stop when Lucas hit his head against the wall hard enough to leave a dent in it. We did it when she wasn't home—Father always let us.

My mother has laugh lines on her forehead and crinkles around her frothy green eyes when she smiles. She has a red birthmark under her left ear that Lucas also has and freckles on her ivory-colored cheeks. Unable to sit for more than thirty minutes at a time, she cleans when she isn't at school teaching math to kindergarteners. That's another trait she gave to me; I don't think I've ever been still in my life.

My father has skin the color of peanut butter with hair and eyes like thunderclouds. He is naturally tall with arms the size of tree trunks and hands so calloused that he's never managed to cut himself with a knife while cooking. Those larger-than-life hands are black with soot at the end of every day from building train engines, which is one of the only jobs we have that requires physical labor, but he enjoys getting to spend time on his feet. I'm like that, too.

"Everyone ready?" my mother asks. "We can catch the early bus so you two can sit with your friends." She smiles nervously—I wonder what this must be like for her, sending the both of us off at once.

"Let's go," Lucas says.

We tug on our boots; he helps me lace mine, as it's hard to bend over in this stupid dress. On any other day, he would tease me about not being able to tie my own shoes, but today is different. Today there is nothing but unspoken kindness in the face of our fear.

Next are our heavy coats, which help me feel a little more dressed. The Matching Ceremony dress code is different than that of everyday life. We don't get to pick our own dresses, but we get fitted for them so they're flattering. I must admit that I look good in this dress—it hugs what little curves I have to offer, with a wide neck to show off my collarbones. This is the first (and probably only) time my male friends will see me like this. I wonder what they'll think of me, if they'll avert their eyes for the sake of remaining proper. I don't know if I want them to or not.

The four of us leave without another word. My father double-checks the lock, as he does every time, and we walk to the bus stop at the end of the street. The Ashborrows are already waiting, thank Ankou.

"Hey," Chris says as we come to stand under the streetlamp with him. "You guys look nice."

"Thanks." I smile bashfully, wondering if he was allowed to say that. "So do you."

"Katie, *wow*," his older sister, Melissa, says. "Wait, can you take off your coat real quick? I wanna see the top."

I shrug off my jacket and hand it to Lucas, offering a little twirl. Melissa whistles and Mrs. Ashborrow nods her approval. As I'd expected, Chris averts his eyes when I look at him. I still don't know whether I want him to or not.

"Stunning," Melissa says, hugging me.

"Thank you," I say, putting my coat back on. "Are you nervous?"

"Not at all," she says. "All packed up. We'll move everything tomorrow. I hope we're near the park. That would be so nice."

Tonight, Melissa and her Match will receive the key to their forever home. The Key Ceremony takes place after Homecoming, when babies are given to their parents for the first time, but before the Matching Ceremony. I think they save ours for last to keep us on our toes.

"Oh, that would be lovely," my mother chimes in. "And not too far either."

"Exactly," Melissa says, wrapping an arm around her own mother. "Can't leave just yet, can I?"

We all laugh as if she ever could.

"Nervous?" Chris asks me quietly.

I look up at him, his eyes piercing my own like ice. "Are you seriously asking me that right now?"

He laughs a little. "Fair. You have any guesses on who you'll get?"

Every year the rumor goes around again that they don't make the list until the day of the actual ceremony, that they observe us in school up until then and pick the best Match that way. I don't know how much I believe that; Melissa's Match was practically a stranger to her.

"Not a clue," I reply. "You?"

"No idea."

The bus arrives, and our families clamber on. As usual, I sit in the back with Lucas and Chris on either side. Our parents and Melissa are up front.

The ride is mostly silent. We stop at one or two other streets, but few people get on. It's still early, only 10:00, and Homecoming doesn't start until 11:00. Why they keep the babies up that late only to send them off to their parents for the first time, I'll never know.

"My mother says I was the easy baby after Homecoming," Chris says as if reading my thoughts. "Mel? She was a nightmare. It took her three days to get back on a semi-normal sleep schedule."

"How do you think our parents felt?" Lucas laughs.

"Oh, yeah," Chris replies, laughing as well.

"I was easy," I chime in, pointing the finger at Lucas. "You? Not so much."

He puts a hand over his heart, feigning injury. "*Me*? But *you're* the one who's still a nightmare!"

I reach over to Chris to swat my brother on the arm, accidentally leaving a little glitter on his jacket as collateral damage. "Oops, sorry, here—" I make to wipe it away, but he grabs my hand, eyes pointed up front.

I follow his gaze to our parents, who are watching us intently. I offer a small wave, returning my hands to my lap.

And just like that, we're at the Hall, and everyone is clambering off the bus. My father offers a hand to every wobbly girl like myself.

As I near the huge wooden doors, I start to count my breaths—1, in, *2*, out. Soon I am mere feet from the inside, and I take my last breath as a free girl.

One last exhale, and then I am inside, shaking so hard I momentarily think my knees might buckle, thankful that I can chalk my tremors up to the cold. I can barely sign my name as I register, only thinking about what could potentially happen to me. The only good outcome would be getting Matched with Noah or Chris, and I would protest even that.

After winding through the outer corridors, we arrive at the Hall itself.

The Hall is a massive dome with seats on all sides and a stage in the middle. The glass roof represents how this is not just an affair for us but the whole country. Anyone could come by to watch, even President Ankou himself. We are out in the open here, at our most vulnerable.

Four main hallways on the floor lead into the cavernous space, so you have to climb to get to the seats. The hallways come in from the north, south, east, and west. Those waiting to be Matched sit in the northeast section, always able to fit because of population control. Young parents are in the northwest, and Matches waiting for their keys are in the southwest. The rest of the population may sit wherever they like, even mingled with those being honored, but they are required to attend.

We take our seats in the designated section; I feel exposed without my parents on either side of me. Some people chatter nervously around us, but our group does not speak.

Finally, Mayor Clearwater steps into the middle of the stage, raven hair rippling around her silver dress like a halo. She taps the mic with perfectly manicured nails to get the crowd's attention

"Welcome, everyone, to this year's Homecoming, Key Ceremony, and Matching Ceremony!" We applaud, and some people cheer. "I'm sure you're all very excited!" We applaud again, most people with even more enthusiasm.

"It's time to begin! Young parents, please come to the front."

We watch as first-timers, beaming with pride, are handed their infants. Some mothers weep with joy; others, it seems, with sorrow. And the second timers look mostly unphased, with a toddler clinging to one of them or sitting on the floor exhausted. The little ones are also required to attend so that a parent doesn't have to stay at home to watch them. It seems cruel.

"And those Matches eagerly awaiting their keys, please come forward!" Mayor Clearwater calls. My leg starts to bounce.

Melissa and her Match receive a home by the park, just like she'd wanted. She beams with pride at her mother and then offers Chris a wave. Then the fateful words.

"And finally, our sacred Matching Ceremony! All girls currently aged 16, please come to the front."

I turn and smile the best I can at Lucas, who sits higher up with his other friends. Tonight, after the Matching, marks the communal birthdate. This year we will turn 17.

I end up standing between Ava and Elizabeth Parker. Elizabeth and I have never gotten along, in the same way that mice and snakes don't. I'm still not sure which of us is which.

"Boys, please come forward and stand opposite the girls," Mayor Clearwater calls. I clench and unclench my sweaty hands. Ava doesn't look much better.

I zone out until Ava is called, and because her last name is only three in front of mine, I start to pay attention.

"Good luck," I whisper. She sends me a half-hearted smile

"Tyler Sandoval, please come to the front," Mayor Clearwater calls. He steps forward, all messy black hair and too-baggy shirt, just as nervous as the rest of us.

"Match necklaces," she instructs. It's a perfect fit, and they both look relatively pleased.

A few more names are called, a few more kids are betrothed, and more than a few panicked thoughts run through my head.

"Kaitlyn Davis." Mayor Clearwater's voice echoes through the silent Hall. "Please step forward." I take a deep breath and step to the middle of the stage, trying to look remotely calm in the face of my future.

"Preston Harper," she reads from the list of names. "Please come forward." Oh *no*. Not him, please, *anyone* but him. I hate him *so* much, and my parents tell me 'hate' is a strong word, but I do. I *hate* him. He shoved me off the top of the playground when we were kids; I still have the scar on my foot to prove it.

Too much gel keeps his hair slicked back, and his dark brown eyes may as well be made of plastic. His behemoth hands are clammy—I can *see* that they are clammy—and the last thing I want is them anywhere near my body. I don't want to marry him. I *can't*.

"Match necklaces," Mayor Clearwater instructs. With shaking

fingertips, I unclasp my necklace and place it next to his. The fit is seamless, with jagged edges coming together to form a perfect heart. My throat aches with unshed tears as we hold up our Match to the crowd's applause. His sweaty rock of a fist crushes my hand.

As other people get betrothed to my best friends and schoolmates, we stand to the side. Noah is Matched with my sort-of-friend Jocelyn, and Chris gets a girl named Danielle. Lucas, always the luckier twin, gets partnered with a good friend of his. Everyone, except me, seems to be somewhat pleased with their Matches.

The rest of the Ceremony goes by in a haze until Mayor Clearwater's farewell speech.

"In this hour, so much has happened! Parents have received their beautiful children; soon-to-be spouses have been gifted the keys to their forever homes. And, of course, our newly Matched citizens have all grown to become fine young men and women," she says, sighing happily and clasping her hands together like a swooning maiden. "Girls have transformed into women; boys have transformed into men. Are you all happy?" We're supposed to chorus a 'yes,' as is tradition, whether we are being truthful or not. Disagreeing can be dangerous.

The air in the room shifts as people suck in a breath. I peer around Preston's mass to see what happened, confused as to why the silence is now suffocating instead of placid. It doesn't take long for my eyes to fall on the mousey girl who has stepped away from her newfound soulmate. "No, I'm not *happy*! I *won't* marry him; I won't! You can't make me!"

Guards rush forward and begin to drag her away, but she keeps yelling and struggling against them. "Let me *go*! I said get *off* me! Mother! Father!"

I can see the fear in her eyes even from here. She knows she's made the wrong choice, but it's too late now.

She's dragged into a small room, and everyone remains silent. Whether we are stunned or indifferent, it is difficult to tell.

The girl screams once, the high-pitched squeal of a pig awaiting slaughter. The unearthly cry is cut short just as it begins by a deafening bang.

All is silent for a final moment, almost picturesque. Many of us still bear the same mask of indifference we plastered to our faces before stepping foot in the building.

Chaos ensues.

Her family sobs, her Match is gaping like a fish, and another member of our crowd tries to run into the room after her. Two guards, looking identical to the others in their black body armor, hold him back.

"Give her back! You have to fix her!" His cries echo around the massive space. "Help her! She's sick; she doesn't know what she's saying! Just help her, *please!* I love her, I love—"

They drag him into a different room, and he doesn't even have time to scream before the gun goes off. This time, there are two shots.

CHAPTER TWO

EVERYONE HAS a different reaction to this horror. Ava is crying silently, Noah doesn't know what to do, and Chris has a hand on Danielle's shoulder. He looks at me with eyes that plainly ask, *'Are you alright?'* I shake my head.

Home? He mouths, and I nod.

Let's go, I mouth.

Someone puts a hand on my shoulder, and I jump a little. "Just me," my mother says. "Ready to go?"

Everyone begins to leave, and Preston walks away without a word, our Match in hand. The men are supposed to hold onto the Match until marriage when we'll hang it above the doorway of our home. Danielle has disappeared, as has Mayor Clearwater and all the guards. Usually, she dismisses us by section, but tonight is very different. Soldiers have killed no civilian in Carcera outside of an execution in 31 years.

"Can I ride with my friends? I'll be home soon," I reply.

"Of course," she says. "Congratulations."

"Thank you," I say formally, forcing a smile onto my lips.

"I'll see you when you get home, alright?"

"Thank you," I repeat as she walks away. I spot Lucas in the crowd and wave him over.

"Hey," he says, hugging me. "You okay?"

"Yeah, fine. I'm just going to ride home with Chris. Wanna come?"

"Sure."

We collect Chris, who says nothing, and then Ava and Noah. Ava weeps silently, and I watch Noah fidget as he tries not to put an arm around her. Noah's always been a hugger, but now he can't touch us in public. We have to save that for our Matches.

Only once we're seated in the back of the bus does anyone speak.

"Congratulations," Noah says quietly to Lucas.

My brother nods, swallowing hard. "Thank you. Lexi's always been a friend… it's nice that I know her."

"I barely know Tyler," Ava says, wiping her cheeks. She sits crammed between Chris and Noah; Lucas stands over the four of us, holding onto the handrail.

"You'll get there," Chris says comfortingly. "I don't really know Danielle, either."

Nobody looks at me. I wonder if it's better to have your Match be a stranger than to have him be a monster.

"Katie…" Noah starts.

"I'm happy," I say quickly, worried about who will hear. "Preston and I… we'll have a good life together."

Chris fidgets next to me, and Lucas is suddenly deeply concerned with the pattern on the floor.

"We will," I say, more for myself than anyone else.

The bus slowly empties as the driver makes several stops. Ava gets off first, then Noah a few stops later. I chalk the quiet up to exhaustion.

Soon it's just Chris, Lucas, and I. We live far from the Hall, but I don't mind. The walk is quite pleasant when the weather is good. And this way, I don't have to see it from my yard or window. I have a nice view of some trees and the school.

The driver lets us off on the corner, and we walk to Chris's house.

"Well," Chris says, clearing his throat and shoving his hands into his pockets. His breath clouds around his face, and he rocks back and forth on his heels.

"Katie, I'll meet you at home," Lucas says, teeth chattering. "Chris, see you tomorrow?"

"Sounds good," Chris replies, and my brother heads off down the street. I am thankful, for the thousandth time, that he knows me so well as to leave me a moment with Chris.

"You okay?" Chris asks.

"Yeah."

"Katie."

I look up at him and frown. I used to think I would protest against being Matched with him or Noah, but now the thought seems like a fairytale in comparison.

"I'm sorry," he says. "It's not... it'll be okay. I know it's not what you wanted, what anyone—"

"I'll be okay," I say quickly. Even in the dead of night, I worry about being overheard. "Preston and I—we—will have a good life."

"I know you will," he says.

"Congratulations about Danielle. She's sweet."

"She is. I just wish—"

"Wishes are for kids," I say, clearing my throat. "Oh, Ankou. Wishes are for kids. We're in real life, now."

He nods. "We are."

We stand in silence for a moment, trying not to shiver. I wonder what he thought of my dress.

"I'll see you tomorrow," he says softly, taking a step back.

I even surprise myself by closing the gap between us and hugging him fiercely, wrapping my arms around his neck, and inhaling his cologne's deep, earthy scent.

"Katie, hey," he says quickly, hugging me back. I feel his breath warm where my collarbone disappears into my neck. "You okay?" he murmurs.

I pull away at last. "Yeah. I'll see you tomorrow."

"See you then."

He turns to walk up his lawn, then stops halfway, turning back to me. "Oh, Katie?"

"Yeah?"

"I like your dress. It's nice."

I grin despite everything that's happened tonight. "Thanks."

He nods and turns away, walking inside his home. My legs carry me down the street, across my lawn, in through the door. I lock it behind me, and they take me upstairs into my bedroom. Flick on the lights, lock this door, and grab my pajamas from the closet. Thank Ankou for autopilot because my mind is, essentially, in the middle of a blizzard. All around me is swirling snow; I'm up to my neck in it. Can't see, can't hear, can't feel.

The sound that slips between my lips is more animal than human. I clap one hand over my mouth as I sit on the edge of my bed, still in my dress, and try not to sob too hard. Abuse between Matches is illegal, but only if you get caught. And even then, even *if* I were able to send him away for a while, he would be back. He would always, *always* be back. Matches of both genders are often eventually killed for reporting their spouse, so most just take the beatings in silence.

The sobs that wrack my body are almost too much to bear. I grow hot and desperately try to rip my dress off—there is a clasp at the back that I cannot reach. My parents are asleep, and I can't see Lucas like this. I rip it off, delighted by the sound of tearing fabric and the popping clasp.

It lies on the floor like a dead animal, and I stand naked over it. The air is cold, thank Ankou, and soothes my burning skin. I feel ill, but there is no food in my body.

Bless my limbs because they work on autopilot again, dressing me in my pajamas and brushing my teeth. There are steady, silent tears on my cheeks, but I wash my face of them anyway. They return only a moment later as I am tucking myself into bed.

Two years. That is what I tell myself as I stare up at the ceiling. Two more years until I no longer watch the shadows of the oak tree climb across it. Two more years until Lucas is not only a wall away, until help is in another building until I am forced to share a bed with the person I hate most. Two more years.

When I wake up, my parents are already making breakfast.

My body dresses, and I arrive downstairs shortly. "Good morning, Mother, Father," I say, trying my best to sound cheerful.

"Good morning, Kaitlyn," my mother says. My parents only call me by my full name because it's what they're supposed to do. The name they gave me at birth is the only thing they can call me, but that rule doesn't apply to anyone else.

"Good morning," I reply. "Thank you for making breakfast."

"That is our role, for two more years, of course," she says, whisking pancake batter. "Don't expect this kind of treatment after the Key Ceremony—Matches don't serve one another this way."

I suck in a breath, not sure what to say. She and my father seem so happy sometimes. Did they ever feel as I do now?

"Hey, Katie." Lucas thumps down the stairs, breaking the tension without even trying. His hair is scruffy and sleep still rests in the corners of his eyes.

"Morning." I smile, the smell of bacon and eggs wafting into my nose.

"Are you pleased with your Match, Kaitlyn?" my father asks calmly, like he hadn't witnessed the murder of two children only hours before. That's my parents—untroubled as always. Then again, I guess that's how all parents have to be.

"Of course, Father," I reply, putting on the familiar mask of indifference. "I feel blessed to be with someone I already know."

My mother side-eyes me but says nothing. She remembers the time I was pushed off the top of the playground, too.

A half hour or so later, after a full breakfast, we have no choice but to discuss the inevitable future. I was once excited about this moment, but now I dread it. My future is now synonymous with Preston's, which has never seemed so bleak.

My mother starts. "You two already know what will happen if—Ankou forbid—you disobey them. You saw it last night, and hopefully, you will be lucky enough not to see it again for a long time."

"But," my father interjects. "That does not mean you are completely safe. One wrong move like those kids last night, and it's over, understand?" Lucas and I nod.

"Good. Now, you two know what's in the attic. If you have questions, you may ask your mother or me in *private*. What is up there is not to be discussed anywhere outside of this house. No one else is to know, not even your cousins or Matches, understood?"

We nod again. The back of my neck grows hot with shame; I've read the whole diary twice and let Ava take little peaks at the more interesting parts. I figured she had the right to see it above anyone else, given what her uncle Victor did.

"I know you might not like hearing this, but you will need to distance yourselves from your friends. Even your friends of the same gender have to survive with a little less attention now that you've all been Matched. Your primary focus must be building a solid relationship with your Match," my mother says.

I know better than to argue, even though it takes all my willpower not to shout about how unfair this is, how my life is being taken from me even though it was never mine to begin with. I resist the urge to sigh and instead focus on keeping my voice placid like they've raised me. "I understand."

And I do; I've been forced to since I could speak. It's the inescapable truth I was born to believe.

"Thank you for understanding, Kaitlyn." My mother smiles, patting my hand gently. After last night, she looks like she's aged 20 years. Guilt tugs at my heart, and suddenly my stomach is in knots.

"Of course." I try my best to smile, then excuse myself to my room to get properly dressed. Delicate snowflakes begin to float to earth like leaves on the lake's surface. This isn't the kind of snow that usually sticks to the ground, but you can never tell. If I've learned anything about snow, it's that you can never predict exactly what it's going to do. It reminds me of people—if you try to guess them, you'll always be wrong.

"Lynn?" Lucas calls, knocking twice on the door. He started calling me Lynn when we were kids because he didn't like my full name, Kaitlyn. He never uses that nickname anymore, but today is different. Everything is different now.

"Come on in," I reply once I'm dressed. The purple sweater—my favorite—covers my collarbone, per the dress code. Women can't show their collarbones around men unless it's their Matching Ceremony, and even that was barely a peek. It's easy in the winter, but summers can be torture.

"Why are you crying?" he asks, closing the door softly.

"I'm not," I snap.

He gently perches at the edge of my bed, bird-like yet somehow very prominent, very *there.* "That's your worst habit."

"I know," I reply with a sniffle. It's impossible to be embarrassed around him. "Can't help myself."

"Figures," he sighs. "You're such a hard-ass on yourself."

"I know," I repeat. "Old habits, right?"

He smiles. "Right. So, what's on your mind?"

"Nothing," I say, fighting the tears. I know that once I let myself break, there will be no re-sealing of the cracks.

He leans over and wipes a tear off my cheek with the sleeve of his sweatshirt, showing it to me. "That is not nothing. Out with it."

"I got Matched." My voice trembles and I hate myself for it. I'm supposed to be strong, not... not whatever *this* is. "I got Matched, Lucas, to Preston Harper. You know what he's like. I can't do this, Ankou, I can't *do* this."

"You're stronger than you think, Katie," he says, voice tender. "And you'll always have me to annoy him if you need me to."

"Thanks," I laugh half-heartedly.

"Anytime." He grins lopsidedly, turning and falling on his back. His head and most of his legs hang over the edge of the bed because he's so tall. I lay back as well, but only my feet and head reach over. We stare at the wall upside-down.

"You're screwed." He starts to laugh. "I mean, I'm not keen on marrying Lexi, but she's at least a good friend. You're totally screwed."

"Unconditionally." I giggle once as if this is the most amusing thing I've ever heard.

Maybe it's because I'm overtired, or perhaps because I've drained myself emotionally. Maybe I don't know what else to do, but I laugh until I fall asleep.

———

WHEN I WAKE UP, it's around one o'clock. Lucas has fallen asleep too, his mouth hanging open, drool on his cheek.

"Lucas," I say, shoving him on the shoulder. My neck aches every time I move. "Get up."

"What?" he mumbles, eyelids pinching together before he opens them. "What do you want?"

"C'mon, I told Chris we'd hang out today," I reply as I stand. The wooden floor is cold on my bare feet, making me shiver.

"He takes the micro-bio course with Mr. Fordson, right?" Lucas asks, and I nod. "Good, I have no idea what the hell a palisade meso-phyll is."

Within 45 minutes, my three best friends sit in my room with us. The snow had stopped, and they all walked here. Ava and Noah live two streets over, and Chris is only a few doors down.

"You guys going?" Noah asks. He bounces a tennis ball against the wall as my parents' voices rise and fall downstairs. I'm supposed to keep my door open all the time to keep airflow circulating evenly through the house—those are my father's words, not mine.

"Going where?" Ava asks. She hardly glances up from her chemistry homework as he repeatedly bounces the ball.

"The funeral," Noah replies. At this point, we all look up from our respective assignments.

"You got a notice?" Lucas asks.

"Yeah, it came in the mail an hour ago," Chris says. "Did any of you know them? I didn't."

18

"I had robotics with the boy," Lucas says. "His name was Levi. And the girl, Natasha, was in my eighth-grade study group for physics."

"I saw Levi around school," Ava offers. "He said, 'hi' to me once."

"Never met either of them," Chris says, rubbing the back of his neck with one hand.

I nod. "Same here. But I still think we should go pay our respects."

"They defied our country, Katie." Ava sits up, and I move with her. "Why should we respect them?"

"Because they said what we were all thinking," I hiss, irritated with her even though she's only saying what she has to. "They were brave."

The remorse vanishes from Ava's eyes—now she just looks pissed. "They were stupid. If you're not careful, the same thing will happen to you."

My jaw tenses. "What does that mean?" The boys are glancing at each other fearfully, wondering what to do. We rarely fight; this is the most heated argument we've had since we were kids.

"It means—" Ava starts but is cut off by a gust of cold air blowing through my window. I always keep it cracked and have for four years.

When I get up to shut it all the way, I notice the guards meandering down the street. Usually, they only patrol just before curfew. Other than that, they hang around outside the school, in the Hall, and maybe by the park.

Sucking in a breath and slamming the window shut, I can't help but wonder if they heard me. Ava wouldn't be in danger, but me... they could kill me. They *would* kill me.

Chris raises an eyebrow curiously. "Everything okay?"

"There are guards down there," I say, glancing back out the window. The two guards turn and prowl down the street again.

"Well, that's... that's not right," Chris murmurs, standing next to me. Lucas looks from Noah to Ava and then to me. The hair on the back of my neck stands up as I watch one of the guards speak into his radio.

"Lucas," I say, even though I already know the answer to my question. "Have Mother and Father said anything for the past five minutes?"

19

When I turn to look at him, he is already halfway down the stairs to find them.

———

CHRIS and I follow Lucas outside, where he is watching the soldiers from the front porch with my parents. Our neighbors across the street are doing the same.

"What's going on?" I ask quietly as we join them.

"We don't know," my mother replies. "Is anyone else in the house?"

"Ava and Noah," Chris says. "Should we go?"

"No, stay," my father says.

My mother nods in agreement. "It would be best to stay here. Do any of you know anything?"

"Nothing," Lucas says, shaking his head.

My mother, always the calmest in tense situations, makes the decision. "The three of you go inside. Let us try to talk to them." She shoos us toward the house, already stepping off the porch. My father follows her as we put on our facades and slip back into the house.

"Katie?" Ava calls from the living room.

I kick off my boots. "Yeah?"

"Just got a public service announcement on the phone," she says, frowning as she walks into the foyer to greet us. "Everyone is to stay inside for the next 24 hours. No one goes to school or work, and those visiting a friend's house must stay there. No exceptions."

"So, the whole town's on lockdown?" Lucas asks worriedly.

"Yeah." Noah runs a hand through his hair. "Looks like you're stuck with us till tomorrow."

"Wow," Chris says. I watch him go through a mental list of times the town's ever been shut down like this. The bank was robbed, a bear got through the train gates, and someone tried to kill his wife and then ran from the guards. Of course, there was a semi-lockdown when the train-design building exploded, but that was just because we were all mourning.

Lucas voices what we're all thinking. "This must be big."

We stand in silence, unsure of what to do next. The wall clock ticks and the furnace whirs back to life, and still, we do not move.

"Who wants to help me get dinner ready?" I ask, finally unable to stand the quiet. Opening the fridge, I take stock of our ingredients. "We have chicken and vegetables."

"I'll help," Ava offers, rolling up her sleeves. "Boys, why don't you call your parents?"

Lucas picks up the phone and tosses it to Chris, who walks into the living room to call his mother. Noah and Lucas wash their hands, then start helping me cut celery and carrots.

Just after Chris hangs up the phone, my parents stomp their way through the front door.

"What's going on?" I ask as they shrug off their coats and kick off their boots.

"They won't tell us," my father says, frowning. "All they said was to stay inside. No work tomorrow, and classes are all canceled."

"Is there any way for us to contact the kids at school?" Lucas asks.

"Why? Who's there?" my mother replies.

"Lexi," he says. It is, quite literally, his job to worry about her now.

"I'm sure they'll be just fine overnight," she says. "Now, where are we at with dinner?"

EVERYTHING GOES SMOOTHLY until the early hours of the morning. The boys sleep in the living room, and Ava shares my bed. She sleep-talks a little, but I don't mind. It feels weird to share a bed with her, though. I haven't slept next to anyone since I was seven or eight, exhausted from a full day at the park. Chris and I fell asleep on the floor at his house, and we only woke up when my father came to carry me home.

The phone rings in the middle of the night, piercing the silence like a gunshot. My mother puts it on speaker as we gather in the living room, wide-eyed and wide awake. Chris and Noah throw their blankets onto the floor to make room for the rest of us to sit stiffly, backs rigid and warm arms pressed together.

21

Warning, a robotic voice says. *Everyone is to stay inside with all doors and windows locked. Alarms may go off, but do not be alarmed.*

"Isn't that the point of an alarm?" Noah says quietly.

Ava elbows him in the ribs. "Shh."

The voice continues. *Alarms are merely a precaution to keep members of the community safe. Remain inside and away from all doors and windows. Thank you for your cooperation.*

The phone clicks off before any of us can touch it. For a moment, there is nothing but silence. Aside from Noah, who can sleep at any time and location, we are all more awake than ever.

"Kids, why don't you go back to sleep?" my mother suggests. I've never heard her voice tremble like this, even when we brought Mrs. Ash borrow food when she couldn't bring herself to the store. "Boys, you can go on up to Lucas's room."

"Thank you, Mrs. Davis," Noah and Chris reply in unison, grabbing their blankets. Lucas leads the way upstairs, and the four of us follow suit.

Exactly fifteen minutes after Ava and I enter my room, I knock three times on the wall. One of the boys replies with four soft taps, and we slip from my room to Lucas's.

His room is messier than mine, despite having the exact same furniture and layout. The bed is a tangle of blankets from which Noah has made a nest, and Lucas's desk chair is shoved into the closet.

"How are you awake?" Noah mumbles, pulling a pillow over his head.

"How can you sleep?" I ask, grabbing one of Lucas's hoodies and pulling it on over my t-shirt. It's colder here than it normally is, and the only light comes from the full moon outside, giving the space an empty feeling despite the presence of five bodies.

"I made coffee earlier," Chris says, handing me a cup. "Four sugars and a lot of milk, right?"

"Thanks," I say, taking a sip. I don't like how bitter coffee can be, but he brews it so it tastes like liquid candy, which is more my style.

"That boy can't make coffee to save his life," Noah complains, tossing a pillow off the bed and rolling onto the floor. "Yet I still drink it." He rises to his knees, grabbing his cup off the dresser.

"Hey, I make it the way people actually like it," Chris says.

"Coffee should be bitter. That's the way nature intended," Noah replies, taking a sip and shuddering. He points to the coffee. "This tastes like a fairy took a piss in it."

"That one literally has just milk," Lucas says.

Noah makes a face, setting it down on the dresser. "Then I'm lactose intolerant."

CHAPTER THREE

I DON'T REMEMBER FALLING asleep, but my mother's worried voice wakes me sometime later. Before I can process what she's saying, I can tell it's bad. Her voice is even more panicked than before, shattering against the walls like glass.

"Kids let's go! We're evacuating to the school; come on."

My head slams against the dresser as I stumble to my feet, groaning as my brain reverberates inside my skull. Lucas has fallen off the bed, and Noah's hair is sticking up on one side. The boys stagger around, pulling on Lucas's sweatshirts and socks as Ava and I grab warm clothes from my room. January in Carcera is brutal, even in broad daylight.

My father holds a lantern high in the hallway so we can all see, and Chris tries to turn on the lamp. It doesn't work. He frowns and tries again, but it stays off.

"They cut the power," my mother explains. "We *have* to go, now!"

We hurry onto the landing, and I duck back into my room to grab Ava a hat. She pulls it onto her head as we thunder down the stairs, fanning around the kitchen to grab shoes and coats. I jump into my boots, tucking my sweatpants inside, and shrug on a jacket. Chris tosses me a hat, which I shove onto my head as we hustle through the front door.

Out in the street, people are running everywhere. The only light is the moon and a dim, fiery glow to the south that outlines the shadow of the Border. Stars ignite the inky blackness above, bigger and brighter than I've ever seen them.

"The school!" my father shouts. "Go to the school!"

"Noah!" Ava shouts as she is shoved to the ground by a faceless bundle of coats running in terror. Noah helps her up and pulls her along behind him.

"Stick together!" my father yells. I take Lucas's hand, letting him guide me through the sea of panicked people. We're not supposed to be outside after curfew; it's one of our strictest laws, one of our most grounding routines.

My mother and father get swept away by the crowd until they're so far behind that all I can see is the dark top of my father's head. I eventually lose sight of that, too. The darkness looms, snaking through the streets even as we chase it away, starlight reflecting off our frantic eyes as we careen around sharp turns.

"Chris!" I shout. He won't be able to hear me over the screaming; there's too much screaming, and my head is pounding.

"Katie!" he yells from up ahead. My eyes scan the crowd, and I eventually spot him up ahead. He's fighting to get to Lucas and me while still moving forward, an impossible task.

I pull Lucas towards him as we turn onto Main Street, joined by more people than I thought lived here. The crowd thickens as my fingertips brush over Chris's. I grab his hand, pulling him closer even as Lucas pulls me away.

"Katie, wait!" Lucas shouts. He stumbles and almost falls but regains his footing at the last moment, and we slam into each other like two storm clouds.

Soon we find our place in the stampede, where we keep a frantic pace all the way to the school. Noah and Ava are not far in front of us, but I still can't find Mother and Father. Could they have gotten hurt in the torrent of people? Are they back at home? Fear turns my knees to water as we race up the hill to the front entrance.

As we reach the doors, the crowd condenses so tightly that I can barely breathe. I am squeezed against Chris's chest—it's warm here.

We make it through the door only a few moments, fanning out again. Suddenly we're pounding down the stairs to the basement, which is the only part of the school I've never at least poked my head into. It's always been strictly off-limits, with two heavy padlocks keeping it secure.

The walls are thick, with a low ceiling that makes me feel claustrophobic. My breath hitches and Chris takes my spare hand when he notices. The icy air and stone send a shiver up my spine. My mother and father are still nowhere to be found; we're on our own as we sit against one of the frigid cement walls, joining Ava and Noah.

Chris's mother and sister are only a few yards away. Ava spots them first, excitedly tapping Chris on the shoulder and pointing until he sees them. He gets up but then remembers that we are all supposed to remain seated to minimize the chaos. Melissa catches my eye and points to my left, and after scanning the crowd, I spot Noah's family.

"Noah, look." I gently shove his shoulder to get his attention. His reaction is similar to Chris's—pure elation. He also gets up before Ava pulls him down, reminding him of the rules. His face quickly turns to worry, and I remember that his brother Owen is sick. Being out in the cold like this won't do him any good, especially being only five.

Ava's older sister Dominique finds us next, waving her whole arm to get our attention. Her family is intact but very far from us. My parents are still missing.

Everyone settles in, huddled together to keep warm, and the quiet falls over the crowd like a warm blanket. Slowly, despite our discomfort, my friends start to fall asleep. Ava is learning on Noah's shoulder, and Chris is against mine. He looks so much younger when he sleeps. I tend to forget how much his father's death aged him.

That was a bad day; there's no other way to describe it. Just bad. We had a community funeral outside the Hall. There wasn't enough time or space to do them privately, nor did we have many bodies to pay tribute to.

We were 11. Chris and I were sitting in my kitchen, eating mac 'n cheese and tortilla chips. He was drinking iced tea. I was drinking lemonade. Lucas and my father were working in the garden, and my mother was washing dishes. The floor shook, and the three of us looked out through the kitchen window as the flames reached for the sky, enveloping the silhouette of the building that had once dominated our skyline.

Chris knew what building it was right away, and he tried to run out the door, yelling, "It's my father; he's there!" He was crying; I'd never seen him cry before. My mother picked him up, all squirming arms and legs as he tried to get away. Lucas rushed inside as per my father's orders, who took off down the street to help.

My mother tried to tell Chris it wasn't his father's building, but we all knew she was lying. Eventually, Chris made it through the back door, and I followed him. He ran towards the fire, even though he probably knew what he would find. I never asked if he did.

I kept pace with him all the way to the front lawn of the building (I was just as fast as him back then). Police and fire trucks were already there, pushing us back in case of another explosion. We sat on the curb and held hands while he cried, watching the curling flames. My father sat next to me at one point to let the paramedics treat the burn on his calf. Chris' mother and sister got there shortly after us and sat on the curb. He cried into his mother's shirt, and his mother cried into his. Melissa, 13 at the time, sat next to me. She took my hand without a word and stared at the smoke as it clouded the pale spring sky.

I don't know how long we sat there, but it was cold despite the heat from the fire. We waited and waited for Chris's father to walk out of the smoke, but he never did. No one did.

The fire still wasn't out by the time my father picked me up and brought me home. Chris bolted to Noah's house as soon as the first charred body was brought out—his cousin, Trevor. He was 18, and I still remember how his mother wailed and tore at her hair.

EMMA GRACE

Ava and I spent most of the following week with Chris and Melissa as our parents helped their mother reinvent her life. We all felt the loss, but not like them. It was a tough week, a tough month, and then a tough year.

Most community members knew someone who had died in the explosion, related by blood or not. At a mandatory speech in the Hall a week later, Mayor Clearwater spoke about 'how beautiful' it was to come together as a community. My skin crawled when she said that.

I'll never forget hearing my parents talk in the kitchen two days after. I was walking downstairs to get a glass of water, but I stopped at the top when I heard them arguing.

"They say there's no cause," my mother said.

"Then how the hell did an entire building blow up?" my father asked. He rarely cursed; I was shocked.

"They still don't know," my mother sighed tiredly.

"I think *they* did it," my father spat. "Crime rates jumped again, and now they're back down. Every time people step outta line, they kill us. It's a scare tactic. I know it is. Can't have a contained bunch of people trying to kill each other."

I stuck my head under the faucet in the bathroom instead.

"WAKE HER UP," Lucas says. I think he's talking about me; I must have fallen asleep. Am I awake now? I don't feel it.

"No, I got her," Chris says. I feel someone wrap their arms underneath me, lifting me off Lucas's shoulder. My neck aches, and my hand grows hot as blood flows back into it.

"You sure?" Lucas asks.

"It's fine," Chris says. "I'll bring her back to your house, then go home."

"Chris." That voice belongs to Preston. It takes most of my half-awake willpower to keep still, painfully still. "Here, I can take her."

"I've got her," Chris says coolly.

"Give her to me," Preston insists. He must want to look good in front of Mayor Clearwater and the guards.

I feel Chris lighten his grip, but he tightens it again after a moment. "Preston, you live on the other side of town. I'm just bringing her to her parents, anyway. Go home."

I relax again as we leave him behind, the rocking motion of Chris's footsteps lulling me back towards sleep.

"I got you," he murmurs. Part of me wants to get up and walk to let him put his hands in his pockets. The other part of me wants to stay here, where I know I'm safe.

After a minute or so of internal wrestling, I whisper, "Put me down."

I hear the smile in his voice as I blink my eyes open. "Okay." He sets me down gently, steadying me as I regain full consciousness.

"Thank you," I say quietly. The crowd around us begins to thin as people stagger up the stairs to return home. We jog with them and emerge into the freezing night, warm breath clouding around our faces. The fiery glow in the south has disappeared, and the east begins to lighten with the rising sun. I wonder how long it'll be before the power comes back. We've never been without it before—not even the explosion knocked it out.

"Don't mention it," he replies. I want to take his hand and hold it on the long walk home, but I can't. Now that we're out of danger, I have no excuse for it.

Settling for shoving my hands into my pockets instead, I continue to look for my parents. I don't see them anywhere, but I'm not afraid anymore. They're fine. They have to be. They'll be waiting in the living room or on the porch.

We walk in silence, with nothing to say. We are all exhausted, stiff, and shivering. Noah and Ava peel off eventually, waving a silent goodbye to Lucas, Chris, and me. The three of us continue on.

"Here," Chris finally says. He pulls off the hat he grabbed from my house and tries to hand it to me as we stop outside his home. His hair is scruffy, sticking up on one side. "This is your father's, I think."

"Keep it," I say, pushing his hand away. How can his fingers still be warm? "I'll see you later."

The ghost of a smile dances across his face. "See you then."

He hesitates before walking away, leaving me in front of his lawn. I can't help but smile as I watch him go, pushing the hat back onto his head and pulling it over the tops of his ears. I watch until Lucas tugs on my arm, and Chris disappears into the shadow of his porch.

Lucas is practically whining as he pulls on my jacket. "Katie, let's go."

Our house is darker and colder than I've ever seen, with empty and barren halls. The front door yawns wide; whoever was last out didn't close it. I can still see my breath inside the front hall, too timid to go much further into the darkness. Lucas pulls open the blinds, letting a bit of natural light inside.

"Mother?" I call. "Father?"

There's no response. Lucas puts a hand on my shoulder from behind, making me jump slightly. "They'll be fine. The danger's passed, Katie."

"I know." I fall onto the rough leather couch in the living room, letting myself sink into the billowy cushions. Lucas sits, too, draping a blanket over me.

"You think everyone made it home safe?" I ask, voice slurred by sleep.

"I'm sure they're all fine," Lucas says. His voice sounds muddled, too. "We're adults now, remember?"

"Yeah." I'm trying to count the nicks on our ceiling to relax.

"Go to sleep," he says quietly, shifting, so he's more comfortable.

The only noise is his endless snoring. Just as I drift off, the wall clock starts to tick again.

CHAPTER FOUR

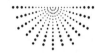

Lucas isn't on the couch when I wake up. My parents are home, but I know better than to ask where they were. They'll either tell me willingly, or I'll never know. The thought of that practically kills me.

They don't say anything when I walk into the kitchen, so I don't say anything, either. Lucas glances over at me, an expression on his face that I know means *to evacuate.*

Mornings in my house can be rough. My mother gets stressed easily, and my father feeds off her emotions. I try to leave home as quickly as possible on mornings like this. Lucas, far more diplomatic than I am, generally tends to stay and help my parents with whatever they're stressed about. We learned the hard way that I tend to get frustrated or bored when I do that. More often than not, it's a combination of the two.

I grab a granola bar from the pantry and jog up the stairs to my room. As I eat 'breakfast,' I call Ava to find out when the funeral is.

"We're meeting at Noah's at 11:30," she says sleepily from the other end of the phone.

I glance at the clock. "It's 10:45."

"Ugh, crap. I might be late."

She hangs up before I can reply.

I only have one outfit appropriate for funerals—we all get the same black skirt and blouse. After some convincing, my hair allows me to pull it into a low bun, but as usual, it requires countless bobby pins.

11:15—time to go.

I slip through the back door, pulling on my nice boots and jacket on the way.

Everyone is waiting for me in front of Noah's house, but it looks like Ava just got there. We all force a pinched smile but don't dare to speak. Talkative as we are, we know right now isn't the time.

The walk to the funeral is silent; there's nothing to say. This will be the first funeral that any of us have attended without our parents and the first for people our age.

The sun shines bright, oblivious to the mood. Even though the light is golden on my face, it gives neither warmth nor joy.

"How could the sun be so bright?" Ava wonders aloud, squinting against the harsh light. "I mean, funerals are about darkness and crying. Why can't it just be cloudy?"

"The way I see it," Chris says. "We only cry at funerals because the deceased are no longer here to provide us with what they have before. It's selfish of us to cry if you think about it, so of course it'll be sunny."

"Hey there, philosophy boy," Noah interjects, half a smile flashing across his face. "Take it easy. This isn't Calla's class."

"Noah," I say, instantly regretting the bite in my voice. I do my best to soften it as I add, "I think everyone should view it however they view it. Maybe Chris is right. Maybe he isn't. I just don't think we should joke about it."

"Point taken," he mumbles, the smile falling from his face. He falls behind a few steps, even though he usually outpaces us all. Guilt pinches in my stomach.

Within the next few minutes, we reach the edge of the forest. Funerals always take place here because the graveyard is outside the Border. We lack the room inside for a bunch of rocks—they say it's better to keep the memories alive in our minds than to focus on death.

We huddle together at the back of the crowd, trying not to shiver too hard. Two mothers and fathers stand in the front, joined by other family and friends, all crying because they'll never be provided with the same person again. They'll never hear the same laugh, see the same face, or feel the same hugs. Maybe Chris was right—crying at one's own loss seems selfish. At least these people get to go on living.

"Here rest Natasha Wilkins and Levi Corpin, both aged 17," the funeral director says. His voice lacks so much as a hint of emotion. "May you be safe and secure wherever you are now. Rest easy, brother, sister, son, and daughter. Wherever you are now, we wish you nothing but joy and prosperity. Know that you are forever loved and cherished here in Carcera. Rest easy."

The crowd echoes back those two simple words, "Rest easy." Now the line forms.

Everyone kisses their left wrist and places it on each casket. It means that if we could've saved them with our blood, we would've opened our wrists and given it to them. It strikes me as odd that they died of (presumably) blood loss and that someone *could've* saved them, but nobody did.

Ava goes first, then Noah. Chris moves into place behind me, and I notice Preston, only a few people behind him.

As I step up to Natasha's casket, his eyes dig into my shoulder blades. I kiss my wrist and place it on the polished wood decorated with pine branches and holly boughs.

Next is Levi's, which is made of darker wood with a rounder finish. His casket has a single paper heart with the words "my son" written in ornate cursive.

"Rest easy," I whisper, pressing my wrist to the wood and moving forward to make room for Chris.

That's all our lives are. All we do is make room for others until there's no room for ourselves anymore. Suddenly we have no room to breathe, laugh, or exist in any other way than surviving each day on its own. And then, before we can even get our bearings, it's over, and we finally rest easy.

I LEAVE the funeral and go straight to school, hoping to make it in time for my robotics class. I always keep a change of clothes in my locker, and so does Noah, so he accompanies me. We talk about physics, his favorite class, and green engineering, which is mine.

The school sits wide atop the only hill in town. What were once gleaming red bricks are now dull and gray, eaten away by countless harsh winters. There's only one school for grades kindergarten through twelve.

Each grade has its own wing, and each group of grades has its own gym and cafeteria. The wings stick out like teeth from a comb, with the gyms and cafeterias making up the main front of the building. There are four divisions of kids, each lasting three years, with the final one lasting four. We're all in the last group—Advanced.

Classes are every day from nine a.m. to five p.m., excluding holidays. My teachers are always there, except for Wednesdays and Sundays, and you can go in for classes whenever you like at least 25 hours a week. We get a schedule every spring and fall for when all the classes begin and end; the only rule is that you can't walk into or out of the middle of a class.

Everyone's still exhausted from last night's ordeal, so there's only one person in the hallway where my locker is located. Noah's gone straight to the cafeteria to get a snack.

I pretend to ignore Preston as I walk to my locker, grabbing my biology and robotics books. When I shut my locker and turn around, I realize ignoring him won't work anymore.

"Hey, Katie." He presses one hand next to my head, forcing me back into my locker.

"Hi, Preston," I say, shifting my books to cover my chest. "Can I help you?"

"We're Matched now," he says, leaning over me, trying to make me cower. I will not tremble; I will not flinch. I am not afraid of him.

"And?"

He raises an eyebrow, looking me up and down, making my skin crawl. I'm still in my funeral clothes, conscious of the fact that I'm wearing a skirt. "Don't you think we should get to know each other?"

"If you touch me today, I will kill you."

His voice is low and calm. If I actually loved him, the sound of it would be reassuring, smooth like caramel sauce. "Does kissing count as touching?"

He presses his lips to mine, heavy and forceful. My books hit the floor with a sound that resembles the gunshots I heard not long ago. After a too-long moment of panic, I bite his lip as hard as I can and shove his chest with both hands.

He yells some string of obscenities, but the sound of my heartbeat is too loud for me to understand. Putting a hand to his bloody lip, he staggers away from me, tripping over my notebooks. Something stops me from running away—I don't know what.

"What're you gonna do?" I say, voice steely calm. "Hit me? You know abuse between Matches gets you up to a year."

"That's not until marriage, and you need to be punished," he says, spitting blood onto the white linoleum floor. The contrast is almost beautiful, and maybe that's why I find myself unable to get out of his way in time. He knocks me to the floor, straddling my stomach and holding my wrists above my head with one hand as the other gropes my chest.

I try to wiggle out from under him, but he's too heavy. "You've been very disrespectful," he mutters. "Make it up to me."

To my horror, he kisses me again, and I can't push him away with my hands pinned like this. I can't even scream.

After more than enough agonizing seconds of his tongue down my throat, the weight is lifted from me. I scramble back against the lockers, lips stinging and chest heaving.

Noah must not have found anything in the cafeteria. Now he's the one straddling Preston, raining down blows on his face and chest.

As he rears back to punch Preston again, I grab his arm and backpedal as hard as I can.

"You don't touch her!" He lands one more blow to Preston's cheek before I completely pull him off. "You don't ever touch her like that again or I swear to Ankou—"

"Noah!" I yell, shoving him backwards.

"He needs to die." Noah tries to push past me, eyes lit like hot coals and locked in on Preston, who lays on the floor groaning like a broken-down bus.

I slam Noah into the locker as hard as I can, making him wince. "Enough!" I shout, and he finally looks at me. "I'm fine. Let's just get him to the nurse, okay?"

"He hurt you," he mutters, pushing his messy hair away from his face, only to have it fall right back over his eyes. "And we can't even tell anyone."

"No, we can't."

"Are you okay? He bruised you."

"I'll be fine. You alright?" I take his hands in mine, examining his raw knuckles.

"I'll live," he says, wincing and pulling away. He steps around me to stand over Preston, who is just now sitting up. "Let's get him to the nurse. We fought, and you found a way to break us up."

If there's one thing Noah's never been afraid of, it's getting in trouble. He and the principal are practically on a first-name basis.

"Deal," I say, standing next to him and looking down at my Match.

Preston looks up at us, spitting blood onto the floor. "You'll pay for this," he says, looking back and forth at us.

Noah leers at him, and he flinches. I smile.

An hour and a half later, after biology and robotics, I'm sitting in my usual hidden corner of the library when I hear the doors slam. The librarian shushes the new arrival.

"Sorry, Mrs. Keily," someone whisper-yells, hurried footsteps clapping on the cool wooden floor. They're coming my way.

I find myself standing up, pressed against the wall; my breath hitches, every muscle in my body tight as wire.

Ava whirls around the corner into my little alcove, and I jump.

"Sorry, Katie," she pants. "Didn't mean to scare you."

"You didn't," I lie as my heartbeat returns to normal.

"We have to do some research," she says, oblivious to my almost-heart-attack.

"On what?" I ask, glancing out of the rows of shelves. The only books I actually read are about green architecture and eco-friendly engineering.

"My uncle Victor," she whispers, turning my blood to ice. He's mad; we all know it. Years ago, when we were little, he started speaking 'gibberish.' He talked about the world outside the Border, the forest and mountains, and the ocean. He said he knew what we really wanted; he knew there were people outside who could free us. Word got out that he was planning a mutiny, and the guards caught him. He's been in prison ever since—the government would have executed him but chose to make an example of him for future generations instead. Only Ava's father is allowed to visit him; his Match killed herself not long after. Ava's father comes home from the visit unable to tell them what happened, but he is more and more upset afterwards every year.

"You do realize this is insanely dangerous, right?" I reply, checking the ceiling for security cameras. Luckily, I find none, but anyone who overhears us has no choice but to turn us in for execution. What we're doing is considered treason.

A smile ghosts across her face. "My father told Dominique everything he said and said when I turn 20, he'll tell me, too. I can't wait any longer, Katie. I have to know if what he said is true."

I pause for a moment, weighing my options. If I get caught, I could die. I think of Preston's weight on my chest, the solid heartbeat I felt pushing into my lower stomach. If I go my whole life knowing that I never even tried to be free of him, I'll die for sure.

I say it before I can think better of it. "Okay."

THERE ARE no answers to our questions. In a way, I'm pleased. No answer means no possibility for a bad one. No answer also means we've hit a dead end. They obviously don't want us to know anything about him or what he said. We can barely even confirm that there *is* an ocean, that it isn't something made up in picture books.

We pack up within the hour, and I arrive home by 5:30 to help my parents cook an early dinner.

We work in silence, like usual. Lucas and I speak via eye contact and slight hand gestures.

Going behind you with a knife.

Okay. Grab the flour?

Got it.

My parents don't even look at us as we move, stoic and placid as ever. I wish—not for the first time—they would show some emotion, just a hint of *something*. After the trauma of the last few days, a hug from my mother would be nice.

Our silence is broken by someone banging like their life depends on it against the back door. I open it with my elbow, and flour dusts the glass by accident. Outside, covered in dirt and dripping wet, is Chris.

"We gotta go," he pants, and my heart drops into my stomach. Something terrible has happened; Chris never panics.

I frown. "Is everything okay?" My family ignores us, used to our friends appearing at the back door at all evening hours.

"Someone heard you," he says as he gets his breath back. "They told the guards. We have to run." Only now do I notice his small backpack slung over one shoulder.

"Where?" I ask, barely hearing myself.

"Outside. Like, outside-outside."

"Chris, we'll die if we try to go out there."

"And the guards are on their way here to arrest you as we speak." He shoos me away. "Katie, they'll kill you."

"Mother, Father, I'll be right back," I say, voice tight.

"Hurry back," Mother says.

Lucas joins me as I race up the stairs. "Where are you going?"

I pause, searching for a lie that is both convincing and legitimate. "I left something at Chris's today. Just gonna go pick it up, and I'll be right back."

"Oh." He stops short. "Well, stay warm." My brother disappears back down the stairs to rejoin my parents. Ankou, I'm leaving my *brother*. We swore this would never happen. I promised.

I grab a warm blanket, my heaviest clothes, and Nana Sophia's diary from under my bed, where I've kept it all these years. My fingers shake as I press an old birthdate letter from Lucas between the pages and zip up my backpack.

Putting on an air of calm, I slip down the stairs, taking water bottles, granola bars, and a few cans of tuna fish from the pantry under the stairs.

I swing my pack onto my shoulders as I pull on my boots. "I left something at Chris's, just gonna walk over and pick it up real quick."

"Be home soon; supper's in 45 minutes," my mother says, and I nearly break down right there.

Before I can, someone knocks on the door.

My stomach drops to the floor as I realize who must be there—guards. They've come for me, for us. They're going to kill us all at an execution outside the Hall for everyone to see. It will be mandatory. Owen—Noah's brother—he will watch me die.

"I'll get it," my father says, opening the door before I can warn him not to.

The guards flood my home like water, pushing past my father even as he protests. Four of them enter the kitchen, one for each of us. My peripheral vision catches Chris pressing himself under the kitchen window, ready to bolt.

"What is the meaning of this?" my father asks angrily.

"Sir, we've received information that your daughter Kaitlyn has been researching past criminals. May we speak with your family?" One of the guards says.

"Lucas, please go upstairs," my mother says. He quickly obliges, giving me a reassuring glance before jogging up the stairs.

"How about we all have a seat?" my mother suggests.

"No, that's quite all right, Mrs. Davis," the same guard says. "I need to know what's been going on in your family. Have you exposed these individuals to any illegal information?"

"How *dare* you accuse my wife—" my father interjects. The guard whips out a pistol and aims it at his forehead. We all freeze, eyes dinner-plate wide.

"Sir, you are straying into a treasonous territory," the guard says quietly.

"Just tell us what you researched, and we'll let you all go," another guard says to me.

My mother's eyes fill with tears as she turns to look at me. "Kaitlyn, please, just tell them what you did. We can fix this."

The tension is palpable—sweat beads on my neck. Seven pairs of eyes rest on me, waiting for an answer. I glance towards the staircase, where Lucas watches me from behind the banister.

Go, he mouths. *Run. Go.*

I glance at my mother and father again, committing this moment to memory just in case. My hand slowly reaches for the back door.

"Don't!" another guard shouts, drawing a pistol. "Hands in the air, Kaitlyn!"

"I'm sorry," I say quietly, glancing at Lucas one more time. He nods at me.

I throw open the back door and leap outside, grabbing Chris's arm and running for my life towards the fence. I am up and over in a moment, thanks to plenty of childhood practice. Will I ever do that again?

Pistol shots echo behind me, but the blood rushing through my ears mutes the sound. We sprint down the street and towards the lake, porch lights snapping on in our wake.

"Where's Ava?" I pant as we cross the tracks, ducking low as bullets whizz overhead.

"The woods!" he shouts, pulling me towards the park. My backpack thumps against my shoulders as we finally make it to cover, darting between the shadowy trees and slipping on patches of ice. Ava and Noah spring up from behind a fallen log and join us.

After what feels like forever, we come face-to-face with the Border. It's so much bigger than it ever seemed; I've never been this close to it. The stone extends upward into the night. Barbed wire is coiled loosely at the top. The cold is sawing at my lungs, and I can almost taste blood.

"How are we going to get out?" Noah pants, panic flashing through his eyes.

"My father's keycard," Chris says, pulling a little piece of plastic out of his pocket. I could kiss him, I'm so relieved.

"It opens the train gates?"

Chris doesn't answer, he just takes off at a dead sprint again. We run along the edge of the Border, following its continuing curve as the twilight darkens into night around us. After a minute or two, we come to a huge metal gate, and Chris swipes his keycard in a slot along the side. The gate shoots upward, silent as a summer breeze. All that awaits us is immeasurable darkness.

"Ready?" Ava pants. We stand side by side, too smart to stay and too scared to go.

"We don't have a choice," I say. "We need to go." I lock hands with her and Chris. She takes Noah's hand on the other side, so we're all connected.

We plunge into the darkness.

CHAPTER FIVE

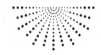

I DON'T REMEMBER EVER RUNNING AS fast as I do now. We tear through the woods at a breakneck speed, only praying we don't fall. Snow and dirt seep through the worn leather of my boots, a freezing slush forming around my waterproof socks.

Sometime after we escape the Border, the exploding pop of machine-gun fire opens up around us.

Blinding lights shine down from above, casting the forest into artificial daylight.

"Duck!" Ava screams.

As we do so, Chris and I leap into a bush, a burst of pain searing my left shoulder.

Ava and Noah duck behind a log, and we scramble to cover ourselves with snow for concealment. Chris holds me tight to his chest as I bite my lip to keep from screaming.

"Are you hurt?" he pants.

"Left shoulder." I force my words through gritted teeth.

"How bad?"

"Just a graze, I think."

We wait, breathing as slowly as we can until the lights give way to darkness and the gunshots fade away. I listen for the echoes of heli-copter blades and gunfire long after they've faded.

Without speaking, we move to sit up. My shoulder protests sharply, and I groan, leaning on my right arm instead.

"We got out," Chris says. "Guys, we made it!" His black hoodie blends into the night so much that I can only distinguish his face and the relief it holds.

"We did," I mumble. I think I'm in some degree of shock, but it's hard to tell. "We made it."

"Katie, you're bleeding," Ava says, worry in her voice.

"Yeah. I am."

"Somebody get out a blanket," Chris orders. "Katie, let me see your arm."

"I'm okay," I say.

"I know you are," Chris says, glancing over at Noah. "We're just gonna take a look to make sure you'll be okay later."

"Okay." I comply and remove my hand from my injury. I didn't notice I put it there in the first place.

Noah wraps a blanket around my other shoulder, which is supposed to help with the shock. I don't feel much difference, only stinging as Chris peels my shirt away from the wound.

I hiss in pain as he wraps it up as fast as possible and vows to take a more thorough look in the daylight. Thank Ankou—no, screw Ankou—that he thought to bring a first-aid kit.

The boys turn their backs as Ava helps me change into warmer clothes. My shoulder burns when I put my arm through the sleeves, but I need to preserve as much body heat as I can if I want to live. But do I even deserve to, now that I've killed the three people I love most?

"Are they alive?" Ava whispers.

I can't answer. "Yours?"

She shrugs. "I hope so."

"You okay?" Noah asks after another moment.

"Yeah," I say, although I feel like I've been run over by a bus. My head is throbbing, my shoulder aches, and my limbs are weights.

We can't stop now; we're too close to the Border. The guards will be back with more helicopters and guns. It's move or die.

Chris frowns slightly. "Okay."

The four of us know—him most of all—that I shouldn't be moving right now. We all know that I have no other choice.

WE JOG IN TWENTY-MINUTE INTERVALS, then walk for ten. I don't know how long we travel that way, but it's a long time. It must be late into the night when we finally can't take it anymore.

"We need to eat," Chris pants. He brushes snow off a fallen tree so we can all sit, which we gratefully do. My legs ache, and my shoulder throbs with every beat of my pounding heart and burns with every ragged breath.

"Agreed," I breathe, leaning on Noah. Ava distributes some half-crushed crackers, and Chris passes around a water bottle. It's not much, but it's food.

"I have apples," Noah says, grabbing the large fruit from his bag and handing one to each of us. I gratefully sink my teeth into it, stomach rumbling greedily. It's the best thing I've ever eaten.

We eat in silence, even nibbling at the cores. Throwing away food we don't like is a luxury we no longer have.

"Is it wrong to be exhausted?" Ava blinks hard to wake herself up.

"No," I yawn, tired now that I feel some semblance of safety. "It's the middle of the night."

"And you need your rest," Noah says to me. "That bullet hole isn't going to heal itself."

"It kind of will..." Chris mumbles, but we all know Noah isn't listening anymore.

"We need to keep going," I say. As I reluctantly move to get up, I hear a sound that makes my blood run even colder than it already is.

"Get down!" Noah yells as the helicopter draws closer. He pulls Ava down by the waist, shielding her from view.

Chris practically tackles me, still taking care not to jostle my shoulder. We crawl to the roots of the fallen tree, which are sticking up in tangles. I wiggle underneath them, helping Ava in behind me. The boys are only half-concealed, covering themselves with mud and snow as the white spotlights sweep over the surrounding forest. All I know to do is pray, but the only person we've been taught to pray to his President Ankou himself, who has brought this upon us.

After what feels like forever, the sound begins to fade. We all sigh with relief and help one another out of the cramped, dirty space.

"That was gross," Ava complains, brushing mud off her jacket.

"It's better than being found." I wince.

"Agreed," Chris says, wiping his face with a look of disgust. I brush some of the extra mud off his cheek with the edge of my sleeve.

We walk for hours, trudging through the powdery snow as the sun rises. Around mid-morning, we finally stop again, this time near a frozen river. I've never seen a real river before; it's wider than I thought it would be.

"Hey," Chris says, coming to a halt. "Cave." He nods towards a small outcropping in the rocks. If I weren't injured, I'd climb to the top of the rocks and look out at the water.

"I'll check inside," Noah replies, advancing slowly towards the darkened alcove. We all hold our breath. An angry, hibernating bear is one of the last things we need right now.

Noah disappears inside and, within a second, yells with a terror-filled voice, "Run! Go!"

"Noah!" Ava screams. We run toward the cave, which is probably the opposite way he wanted us to go.

We stagger into the cave, unused to stepping on stone instead of snow.

To our surprise—and relief—there's no bear, only Noah laughing hysterically.

"You should've seen your faces!" He laughs wildly, holding his stomach. "That was priceless!"

"You *ass!*" Ava yells, packing a snowball and throwing it at him. It hits him square in the face, and he wipes some of it away with the sleeve of his jacket.

The three of us sarcastically roll our eyes, relaxing a bit despite the situation.

"Ava and I can go grab firewood while you guys set up camp," Chris says, bringing us back to our harsh reality.

"Why do I have to get firewood?" Ava nearly whines.

Chris points at Noah. "He gets to do the boring things for scaring us like that."

Noah scoffs, pressing a hand to his chest as if to say, *'how dare you?'*

"And she,"—Chris pauses to point at me— "has a bullet wound."

"Fine," Ava grumbles. Chris hands his bag to Noah, says something under his breath, and walks into the brightness again. The sun is high in the sky, but the days feel impossibly short this time of year.

"What'd he tell you?" I ask.

"Nothing."

"Okay."

"What?"

"Nothing." I sigh as I pull out the blankets. "We need a plan."

"Chris'll know what to do," he says reassuringly. "He always does."

That's a lie; how could he? We've never been in this kind of mess before. Fortunately for us, the plan we desperately need comes to me at the right moment. Richard, Nana Sophia's boyfriend, had family who lived in a nearby city called Pevidere. I remember reading about how they went there once; maybe there's something in the diary that can help us get there.

"Look," I say, pulling out Nana Sophia's diary. "Pevidere was decimated, remember? Bombs and everything, but some of the buildings were still partially intact."

"We ran north," Noah replies. "The ruins of Pevidere are south of Carcera."

I point to the mouth of the cave while my eyes skim the pages. "That river is the Fluvera; it passes Carcera a few miles to the east, far enough away that we'll be safe. If we follow that, it should lead us right there within a few days."

"Do we have enough to last a few days?" He asks, looking at our meager supplies with a grim expression.

"Noah, we don't have enough supplies for more than a week," I say. Why can't he find the ability to see my plan? "If we make it there, then at least we'll have adequate shelter. We can't survive if we stay out here, and there could be food."

"That food is hundreds of years old," he points out.

I sigh huffily. "It's better than no food."

"Good point."

"You in?"

"Do we have any other choice?"

Luckily, Noah backs me up when I pitch the idea to Ava and Chris. They're doubtful at first, just like he was, but they come around. Chris rewraps my wound, cleaning it out the best he can without getting water all over me.

When we're done, we sit in silence. Our families are dead, we're outside the Border, and we can never go home again. Twenty-four hours ago, I was in school, in robotics class, wearing jeans and my favorite sweater and drinking tea from the cafeteria. Now I am in a cave, shivering, and I've been shot. There is nothing to say. I vaguely register Noah sniffling, but we all pretend it's because of the cold.

"We should rise early," Chris finally says, glancing outside at the sky. The sun is only about midway through the sky, but we're all exhausted. "Head out as soon as the sun rises."

Noah nods, adding a few sticks to the fire. It crackles, warming my face as I inhale the crisp scent of burning pine. The excess smoke is almost too much to breathe, but some of it drifts through a small hole in the ceiling. I can't believe Noah had a lighter in his bag.

"We should take watches," Ava suggests. "Two-hour shifts?"

"I'll go first," Chris offers as we pull out our blankets. "You guys get some rest."

"Wake me up in two hours," I say. He needs sleep just as much as the rest of us, whether he thinks that or not.

"Got it," he says, but I can tell he won't. Chris is often too selfless for his own good.

I settle down next to Ava, sharing our two blankets to conserve warmth. Noah rests about a foot away, taking Ava's hand and using his other arm as a pillow. I lay on my back, staring up at the hole in the ceiling through which tree branches are just visible against the sky.

The last thing I see is Chris staring at the sky as if it had answers.

MY EYES FLY OPEN SOMETIME AFTER dark. Chris flicks his gaze toward me, jumping a bit at the same time as I do.

"You alright?" he asks. It's cold, colder than I would've thought possible, and I long for the now-dead fire.

Chris speaks again before I can ask. "It's so clear tonight; I didn't want anyone looking for us to see the smoke. And the light, of course."

"Right," I reply, sitting up and brushing the hair away from my face.

"You okay?" he repeats.

I nod. "Fine."

He shakes his head, patting the stone next to him. I tuck the corner of the blankets under Ava's shoulder and move over next to him. Sitting against the wall with him, I let him wrap part of his blanket around my shoulders. The beds of my fingernails ache from the cold, and it hurts just to breathe.

"Talk to me," he says quietly, pressing his side against mine. I convince myself it's just to share body heat.

"I honestly can't even remember what it was." I sigh, rubbing my temples. "Lucas was there."

"I'm sorry," he says, taking my hand. His hand is remarkably warm for the weather, or maybe mine is extra cold. "You wanna go back to sleep?"

"Not really." I glance through the hole in the ceiling once again. Now I can't even see the tree branches, but I know they're there. "Chris, what *happened*?"

He sighs. "Like I said, someone overheard you and Ava. They knew Ava by voice and reported her. When the guards showed up at her house, her parents met them at the door. You know her father—"

"There's no getting past him," I say, smiling faintly.

He chuckles. "Yeah. Well, they stopped the guards at the door, and Ava bolted. She ran to my house, freaking out. Mel... Mel gave her some clothes so that she wouldn't be cold. The plan was just to lay low in the park or something, pray everything would blow over, but then they knocked on my door, too. That's when I knew that if they connected the dots to me, they'd be at your house any second. My mother stalled while I packed a bag, and Ava ran to Noah's while I went to your house."

He says it surgically, each word falling perfectly after the other as if they'd been revised a hundred times. I wonder if he'd practiced them in his head, waiting for me to ask.

"What did we just do?" I whisper.

He shakes his head, swallowing hard. "I don't know. Do you think..."

I nod, trying not to cry. "Yeah. Yeah."

"I'm so... Katie, I'm—"

"Don't say it," I say, practically begging. "Please, don't tell me you're sorry. You've lost as much as me."

"Okay."

We sit in silence for a long while, each letting out the occasional sniffle as we try not to sob in front of one another. I miss my bed, my pillows, and the sound of my father snoring through the wall. He's supposed to be snoring on the other side of the wall.

"Is it alright if I sleep?" he asks softly, obviously exhausted. Of course, he is; he hasn't slept since well before we left. Left, ran, were forced away—I don't even know how to describe this mess we're in.

"Of course," I say.

He lays down, using my thigh for a pillow. His breathing deepens within minutes, and I smile. Comforted by his presence, I also can't help but fall asleep.

WHEN I WAKE UP, Chris and Noah are gone. Ava is awake, opening a sleeve of crackers for breakfast.

"Nice to see you join us," she jokes, handing me about ten crackers. "Eat up."

"Where are the boys?" I ask, rubbing my eyes and pulling out a water bottle.

"Out for more firewood," she says, with air quotes. "I think they're talking about you."

"What?" I cough, and the crumbs catch in my throat. "Why?"

"Health reasons, probably." She shrugs. "I don't know. Noah was giggling when he saw you and Chris earlier." She grins knowingly; Ava knows everything about everyone.

"That?" I ask, feigning nonchalance. "That was nothing. Chris woke me up when it was my turn for watch."

"Uh-huh."

"Leave me alone," I groan, covering my eyes against the brightness of the snow.

She pops a cracker into her mouth, chewing and swallowing it before continuing. "Never. But seriously, what happened last night?"

"I just... woke up." I shrug. "Said I would take watch; he said okay and fell asleep. That's it, end of story."

"Sure," she says.

"What?" I exclaim.

"*Nothing.*" She knows me better than I know myself—sometimes it's scary. "Come on, let's go. They're bound to be back soon."

"What're we doing?" I ask, rubbing my eyes. My shoulder burns as I stand, but I do my best to ignore it.

"You okay?" she asks, ignoring my words.

"I'm fine. What're we doing?"

"Cleaning up and taking inventory," she says, and I groan under my breath. "What was that?" She crosses her arms and arches an eyebrow in that special way that makes you feel like you've done something wrong even if you haven't.

I roll the blankets and distribute them between our backpacks as Ava organizes our food and water.

"It's not much, is it?" I say, seeing her look of dismay.

"Half a loaf of bread, three water bottles, two sleeves of crackers, half a jar of peanut butter, three granola bars, two cans of tuna fish, and three apples," she says quietly. I cringe—that's hardly enough for two days, let alone forever.

"We should set a few traps at our next spot," I say. "Catch small things, if there is anything."

"Fishing, maybe," she suggests.

"It could work." I nod skeptically, placing our packs in a row at the back of the cave and glancing outside again. "Boys better get back soon."

We sit in silence for a few minutes, left with nothing but our thoughts until Noah and Chris return. I think primarily of my mother, who would know how to keep everyone safe in a time like this, fed, warm, and in good spirits.

"There," Ava finally says, standing up and wading out into the freshly fallen snow. I step in her tracks to make it a bit easier, holding my left arm to my chest to keep it still.

"Hey!" Noah waves. The sound of his voice is deafening in the white silence of the forest.

"Where have you been?" Ava asks, trudging the rest of the way in a somewhat-elegant jog. Somehow, she's still more graceful than me, despite being two inches shorter and in boots that are half a size too large.

"No firewood?" I ask, raising my eyebrows.

Chris's cheeks are flushed pink. "Nothing dry. We ready to start following the river south?"

"Prepped for launch," Ava confirms. She tracks snow into the cave, and I'm reminded how my mother always made us take off our boots at the door. Homesickness feels like a punch to the gut—I've never felt anything like this before.

"Good." Chris glances toward my shoulder, voice low. "Are you alright?"

"I'm fine," I lie. "Are you?"

"I'm fine," he echoes, brow furrowing in worry. I mirror his expression as he reaches one hand up to my face, ghosting over my forehead with the back of his hand.

"We're going to have to change your bandages," he mutters.

I nod, mouth suddenly dry and stale. I can feel my heart pounding in my chest, ears, and throat. Oh, Ankou, I miss my toothbrush.

Chris stares at me for another moment and then walks away, leaving me shivering. My stomach is a mess; why am I nauseous? Ava and I glance at one another, and she winks.

I roll my eyes, slinging my backpack onto my good shoulder. "Let's go." I lead the way out of the cave and try to distract myself from how much I sound like Lucas.

AFTER SOME THOROUGH investigation late in the afternoon, Noah discovers that we can walk across the river if need be. During a break, Ava tentatively steps one doll-like foot on the ice, holding her breath.

"It held me," Noah says, scooping up a handful of snow and biting into it. I cringe and look back at Ava, who is now standing about three feet from the shore.

"You're a twig, Noah," she says, keeping her feet light. "I'm not."

"Ava, the only fat on you is your butt," I joke; Chris is mortified. "What? I'm not lying."

He remains silent, cheeks pink from the cold and a little red from embarrassment. Back home, we weren't allowed to say things like that in front of boys. But for the first time in our lives, we're not home.

Noah takes my comment much lighter, choosing to laugh instead of gape.

Ava giggles, putting a hand on her hip. "It's true—I've got that ballerina booty."

Even Chris lets out a small chuckle at this.

Noah steps onto the ice, offering her a hand and bowing. "May I have this dance?"

"It would be my pleasure," she replies, taking his hand. He twirls her first, stepping out onto the smoother ice. She stands on her toes, boots spinning fluidly. Her eyes light up in a way they haven't in a long, long time.

The strong sunlight bounces off the ice, and they're practically glowing as he twirls her into him. They twirl and slip and grab each other for balance, laughing against the backdrop of blue sky and royally green pines. He dips her, and she throws her head back, long black hair skimming the ice for just a moment. Ava snaps back up, detangling herself from him and dancing back to us in a series of pirouettes and leaps. She is a beautiful machine, fluid with the kind of grace you rarely see in human form.

She stops in front of Chris and me, curtsying with perfect form. As I begin to clap, I notice that she's gotten much farther from the shore. Before I can tell her to be careful, the ice beneath her feet begins to crack.

CHAPTER SIX

"Ava!" I shout. Noah runs toward her but slips, barely catching himself before smashing his head into the ice.

Ava stares at us as if expecting an answer, frozen in motion with eyes wider than dinner plates.

"Don't move!" Chris shouts. "We're going to get you both a tree branch. Stay exactly where you are, and *do not shift your weight.*"

"O-okay." Ava's breath catches in her throat.

"Breathe even," Noah says, lifting one foot off the ice. It groans under the changing of his weight, prompting Ava to exhale just as quickly. "Even, Ava." He sets his foot down slowly, inching his way toward her. Chris scrambles around for a tree branch that he can break, but most of them are too tough or too thick.

"Chris, there's no time," I say. The fissures open wider, spreading towards them. "Guys, you need to start walking toward us."

"I can't," Ava whines. Even as she speaks, the ice cracks more. "Noah, go to shore."

"Not without you," he says. The ice groans, beginning to give way under him as he takes a few more shuffling steps.

"Noah, *go!*" Ava cries, reaching a hand toward him.

"No," he grunts, reaching back to her. Their arms fall just short.

Chris finally extends a branch, but that too falls short by a few measly feet. "Jump for it. I'll pull you in," he practically begs.

Noah glances at Ava, catching her eye and nodding reassuringly. "Do it. I'll be fine."

"Not without you," she echoes. "I'm not leaving this ice without you."

I know what's going to happen moments before it does. *"Noah!"* My cry comes too late; he leaps toward her, catching her around the waist and throwing her toward shore. The ice shatters upon impact, plunging him into the freezing water below.

Finally, my legs remember how to move, and I run onto the stable part of the ice.

"Noah!" Ava screams, scrambling away from the yawning hole on her hands. Chris picks her up and helps her to shore before joining me.

Most pieces of the ice are filmy and breakable, narrowing our options. I spot a solid piece and hop over to it, almost losing my balance and falling into the water.

We reach the gaping hole where Noah fell in, but he's nowhere to be seen. I rip off my jacket and throw it to Chris, gritting my teeth to keep from crying out from the pain in my shoulder.

"Katie, let me—" Chris starts.

"You're more important," I say, tucking my hair back as I prepare to dive in. I glance up at him as the ice groans under my knees. "We all know it."

I plunge into the murky depths before he can argue, but I immediately gasp in shock, and my mouth fills with water. The river is deeper than I imagined, darker than I would've thought possible. I force my eyes open, but they burn from the cold. Noah is a few feet away, sinking fast to the bottom. My strokes are awkward and uneven, and it's hard to tell if I'm getting anywhere. The current is pulling him under the ice that I'll never be able to break.

Finally, as my lungs start to ache with my heartbeat, I grasp the edge of his jacket between my fingertips. The edges of my vision start to go dark as I near the surface. The sky looks so blue through the ice, distorted yet crystalline. I punch the ice above me, shoulder screaming in pain. There—a weak spot. I push through, sucking in air and coughing as strong hands grab hold of me.

Somehow, I get the words out over my relentless coughing as I pull Noah's head above water. "I got him."

Chris hauls him onto the ice, then turns to help me out as well.

I lie on the ice and suck in air as Chris rolls Noah onto his side, hitting him on the back.

"C'mon, Noah, breathe. C'mon, c'mon."

After another moment of terrifying silence, Noah coughs, wet and gurgling. Water spews from his mouth, and I nearly sob with relief.

Noah, coughing less violently now, pushes himself up to a seated position.

"Oh, Ankou." Chris engulfs him in a hug so tight it looks like he'll break his ribs. Noah hugs him back, holding onto his best friend like a lifeline.

"I thought you were dead. You're bleeding."

"I'm okay." Noah pushes Chris's worried hands away from his face.

"Can you walk?" Chris asks, looking dubious when Noah nods without hesitation. "Katie, can you?"

"Pretty sure," I reply. Chris stands first, giving me a hand and then offering it to Noah. He rises carefully, knees visibly shaking. Chris puts an arm around his shoulder to steady him, and I support him on the other side as we pick our way back to shore. Once there, Ava engulfs the two of us in blankets, muttering some choice insults of gratitude under her breath.

The smile of relief falls from her face after a moment or two. "Thank you," she says shakily, blinking hard.

"Anytime," he says, hugging her tightly.

"Alright, let's get outta here." Chris smiles halfheartedly. "You guys alright?"

"I'm good," Noah replies, glancing over at me. "Y-you?"

"All g-good," I say, desperately trying to force away the chills shaking my body.

"Noah, you okay?" Ava asks worriedly.

"I'm f-fine," Noah says as shivers wrack his frame.

"Oh, shit," Chris mutters, shrugging off his jacket. "Everyone, take off your clothes."

"S-sorry, what?" Noah says as Ava and I gape.

"You guys didn't take that unit with Mr. Young. I forgot," Chris says, pulling off his hoodie as he speaks. "You two need to get out of those clothes, or you'll freeze. The only way to keep you warm is to get close, I'm sorry. We have two girls and two boys; it all works out. I'll sit with Noah and Katie. You sit go with Ava. We have six blankets, three for each pair. Take off all your clothes but leave your underwear on."

"Oh, Ankou," I mutter, rolling my eyes even though this might save our lives.

It hurts to pull my hoodie off, and getting out of my thermals is just plain challenging. My jeans peel off, pale legs underneath covered in bruises.

Ava hesitates, poised to take her tank top off. "I didn't wear a cute bra."

"Wear whatever you're comfortable with," Chris says. "It'll probably work better if you expose as much skin as possible, but I'm not going to make you do anything."

Ava pulls her tank top up over her head. "We're all friends here."

Soon we're all standing in a small patch of cleared land, shivering half to death with our clothes laid out on our packs so the sun can dry them.

"Three blankets each," Chris says, handing Ave three blankets with shaking hands. Noah's lips are turning blue, and he can't even find the energy to stand up straight.

"Put one on the ground first," Chris instructs. "Lay on that, then get as close as possible. Pull the other two around you in a kind of cocoon."

"Alright then," Ava says. "Sounds like a plan."

She lays one blanket on the ground, the longest one, and sits down on it. "I don't know how you wanna do this, Katie, but it's gonna be pretty awkward no matter what. We're either spooning, or your face is dangerously close to my boobs."

"I'll go with option one, thanks," I say, lying down next to her and curling into a ball.

"Dammit, Katie, I wanted to be the little spoon," Ava complains.

"Who jumped in the river?" I joke, tucking the blanket under my legs and shoulder, then reaching around to pass it to her. She does the same with the other blanket, and then we pull the bottom blanket up and tuck the edges in. If a helicopter were to spot us, there would be no way we could run away fast enough.

"You guys good?" Chris asks, looking over at me. He can barely meet my eyes over Noah's head from where he is.

"Yep." I am unable to keep the smile off my face at the sight of the boys. Their outer blanket is bright magenta, and Noah is curled into the smallest ball possible. Chris has his entire body wrapped around him, Noah's soggy hair in his face.

"What about you?" I ask him as Ava wraps her arm around my stomach, trying her best not to touch my shoulder. Chris was right; I already feel much warmer.

"Chris is a terrible big spoon," Noah mutters, eyes closed.

"We're not in this to be cute, Noah," Chris jokes.

"Speak for yourself," Noah grumbles, sighing once. I can tell the moment he falls asleep. I follow not long after.

WE WAKE as the sun begins to set, changing back into our heavy clothes and finding a small rock outcropping to camp beneath for the night. We have no energy and no dry wood for a fire, so we huddle up, split a can of tuna fish and some slices of bread, and fall asleep with grumbling stomachs.

The following day we're up before the sun, and we decide to skip breakfast despite the gnawing in our stomachs.

Nothing moves in this silent forest, no wind, no animals, no clouds. Only the still stars overhead, so big they seem to have teeth.

We wind between thick stands of pine and boulders the size of small houses, searching for signs of animal prints while on our way south. There is, of course, nothing. If I didn't know better, I would say that we are the only things left in the world.

As expected, Noah is the one to break the silence, shattering it like a pane of glass. It reminds me of the windows in my house when they were hit with bullets less than three days ago. How could so little time pass between then and now? It feels like years.

"How many days do you think we have?" Noah asks. He leads us through the endless expanse of pine trees as the sky lightens to a violet blue.

"What do you mean?" Ava replies from behind me.

"To live," he says bluntly. I am silent, stunned by his straightforwardness once again. By now, I doubt that I'll ever get used to it.

"Well, we have at least two more days of rations," Chris begins. "And—"

"Don't," I snap.

"You okay?" Ava asks curiously.

"Fine." I focus on walking in Chris's footsteps and blinking away tears. I don't want them to know how weak I really am. I must be strong if I'm going to survive out here; there is no room for weakness.

"That's believable."

I can tell she's rolling her eyes. I don't reply.

We march on for a few more minutes, the tension palpable. It's so cold that I can see the humidity of my breath crystallizing in the air.

This time, it is Chris who speaks up first. "So, what now?"

Noah shrugs. "I don't know. We're going south, right?"

"Yeah," Chris replies. "As long as the river's going south, which it seems to be."

"Seems to be?" Ava asks doubtfully.

"It's a bit difficult to tell without a compass," Chris replies. "We could be drifting east or west a bit, but the river doesn't seem to curve too much, so we should be okay."

"Should be," I mutter, half-laughing. We *should* be going south. I *should* want to live… I feel like I don't know anything anymore.

"Are you okay?" he snaps, stopping short and turning to face me.

"Well, that's a stupid question."

"Why?"

"I don't know Chris, maybe because my parents and my brother are... got shot, because of me. Maybe that's why I'm in a crappy mood."

"That happened to all of us."

"Yes, I'm very much aware."

We stalemate for a moment, staring at one another as the sun rises and the world turns.

Chris melts first, glacial eyes softening into puddles. "It's not your fault, Katie." He peers around me to look at Ava, who has been sniffling all morning intermittently. "Or yours. You did not do anything that should've resulted in... in what happened."

"Neither did Natasha and Levi," I say.

"Or Victor," Ava says quietly.

"Or Victor," Chris echoes. "Listen, if... if anything he said is true, we need to keep moving." He turns to look at Noah, too, looking back and forth between all of us. "We've got to see if he was right, okay?"

Noah, Ava, and I all nod, too choked up to speak. We continue to trudge through the endless forest in silence. Ava sniffles, and I do, too.

THE NEXT THREE days pass the same way. We barely speak to one another, just beginning to process the unfathomable nightmare we're living. We are cold, always, and we sleep in a large pile to stay warm. Noah shivers the most, as if he never quite dried from the river. My arm aches, Ava's back hurts, and Chris speaks only once or twice daily.

Late in the afternoon, on what feels like the thousandth day, we finally make it to Pevidere.

"Wow," I breathe, coming to stand near the edge of a cliff. We'd left the river behind hours prior, climbing endlessly up to see if we could get a view of our surroundings. Our toils paid off.

The sun is just beginning to cross over to the west, the destroyed city resting in the valley below. The ruins stand like skeletons, silent where there once must've been so much noise. We've never seen anything like this place, buildings so tall it looks like they could scrape the clouds right out of the sky.

"Guys, look," Noah says, turning in a slow circle.

I turn with him, taking in the wild landscape. The river we were following flows through Pevidere and into the mountains beyond. We can see all the way to the distant place where the clouds touch the earth, so far away it's unimaginable. I never thought the sky could actually make contact with the earth; we were taught they were always separate at school.

"It's so big," Ava whispers, tipping her head back to the sky and inhaling deeply.

"Endless," I marvel, looking down towards the bottom of the cliff. The drop-off is sharp and steep, and the rocks below look miles away.

"So, we going?" Noah grins. It's the first time one of us has smiled in days.

"Where else is there to go?" Chris grumbles, the hungriest of all of us.

"Hey, chin up," Ava says, nudging his arm. "A win's a win."

"She's right," Noah says. "And I don't say that often."

We all laugh a bit because he's right. Even Chris cracks a smile.

"So, come on," Noah finally says, starting down the mountain. "I'm hungry."

CHAPTER SEVEN

My breath catches in my chest as we step into the city. *Wow.*

The stone underfoot feels unnaturally solid after trudging through muddy slush for so long. The buildings tower over us—most of them are decorated with shattered windows, and huge chunks of metal litter the streets.

"It's huge." Chris tilts his head back in wonder.

"It's so quiet," Noah murmurs.

"Do you think they're still here?" Ava whispers.

"Everyone died," I say. "It said so in the diary. The government executed the whole city—they were traitors."

"Katie, that's not what she means," Noah says quietly. I shiver once I realize that they're talking about the bodies.

Chris reassures her. "There's no way the government would just leave them here. Even they aren't that cruel."

I'm not sure I believe him as we step into one of the buildings. The doors were blown off, leaving a gaping wound in the framework. Inside, metal chairs have been thrown everywhere, shards of glass littering the floor.

"Watch yourself," I say, nodding towards the glass. "It's probably still sharp."

"Look," Chris says urgently. He strides over to a large circular desk littered with ancient computers and corded phones.

I move with him, looking down at the computers and keyboards. "Wow. That's *old*."

"No kidding. This is a hospital; there might still be medical supplies around." He pauses for a moment before remembering that we might not be sure exactly what he wants. "We're looking for sling, bandages, blankets, and dry clothes. I say we spread out and start looking."

"And if we get lost?" Noah asks.

"There are directory signs all over, see?" Chris points to an arrow that says *ICU*. "I'll head there for blankets. Ava, you hit the ER for medical supplies. Katie, look for clothes in the... psychiatric ward, whatever that is. Noah, can you go with Katie? She's only got one working arm."

"Both of my arms work just fine, thank you very much," I grumble even though I'm glad to have the company.

"Meet back here in an hour," Chris says, glancing at the clock even though it isn't working. He looks at his watch instead. "Yeah, an hour is good."

Noah and I head off to the psychiatric ward while Chris and Ava go entirely different directions. It's lonely not to have everyone right next to me, even with Noah here.

We meander through the halls, staring at broken beds and doors blown off their hinges. Chris was right—this whole hospital was emptied.

Things take a different turn when we make it to the psychiatric ward. Each door has a keypad and a place to swipe your ID. Of course, the doors are swinging on their hinges, so it doesn't matter much.

We rifle through the cabinets in one room, and I glance out the window. What was once a clear blue sky has now been replaced by a sheet of clouds. Snow is beginning to fall, thick and heavy. There must be a massive storm on the way.

Noah ducks his head to peek outside. "Yeah. Good thing we made it here. We'd be dead if we got caught in that."

Something clatters in the hallway, and my stomach drops.

"Behind me," Noah murmurs, already pushing me back there. Not for the first time, I appreciate his protectiveness, although I'm slightly insulted that he doesn't think I can take care of myself.

"Hello?" he calls out. We stand frozen, waiting for a response.

A man appears in the doorway, and Noah steps back into me. I stumble, trying to put my left arm out for balance and practically yelping in pain.

"I'm not here to hurt you," the man says, although he's holding a gun.

"Back up," Noah growls, balling his fists.

"It's okay."

"I said *back up*."

The man kneels slowly, placing his gun on the floor, and then raises his hands as he stands back up. "Really, it's okay. I'm here to help you."

I realize how deranged we must look, covered in mud, blood, and frost, clutching dirty backpacks and moth-bitten blankets.

"Noah," I say quietly. "Maybe he's right."

Noah glances over his shoulder at me, and that's all it takes for the man to spring forward, grabbing him and pinning his arms behind his back.

"Noah!" I scream, reaching for him, but the man turns his back. Noah bucks and struggles, throwing his weight around as the man hangs on. I rain down blows with my good arm, but it isn't enough.

I look wildly around and then settle on the knees, kicking the man as hard as I can. He stumbles and falls, dragging Noah with him. They struggle on the ground for a moment as I grab a piece of what was once a chair and slam it down on the man's head.

He falls limp, too limp, and Noah rolls away. Blood trickles onto the floor from a gash I opened up in his temple.

"Holy shit," Noah pants, sitting back on his knees. "Shit. Chris and Ava."

I stare at him with wide eyes, still carrying my makeshift club. "Shit."

I am faintly aware of the burning in my arm as we sprint from the room, careening down the hallway and desperately searching for the stairs we took to get up here.

"Ava!" Noah screams, pausing in the middle of a hallway to whip his head around, eyes wide with panic. "Ava!"

I shove him, and his rolling eyes find mine. "Noah, quiet! There are more."

"Shit," he pants, running a hand through his hair. "Okay, okay. Ava's in the ER, Chris is in the ICU."

"ER is gonna be on the first floor," I say. "Let's go there first. Chris is more likely to fight someone off."

He nods, and we start a quiet jog down the hall, still searching for a stairwell. Eventually, we find one; by now, even the fingertips of my left hand are throbbing.

"Noah," I breathe as we come to the first floor.

"Yeah?" He turns over his shoulder to look at me before shoving the door open.

"Can I stay with you?"

"As if I'd leave you. C'mon."

The lobby is eerily silent. Snow floats down outside, muffling the whole world, and there is no wind.

Noah shoots his arm out, stopping me from walking forward. "Look," he whispers, nodding to the far corner. A boot pokes out from behind an overturned desk—Ava's boot.

I press my good hand over my mouth to stop from screaming—oh, Ankou, tell me she isn't dead.

Noah drops to the floor, and I follow suit before I even register that two people are standing near Ava. We crouch behind some over-turned chairs and a hunk of rubble as they talk about her.

"She must be from Carcera," Person One says.

"How? No one escapes from there," Person Two replies.

"Where else would she be from? She's fairly clean, clothed, and well-fed. There's nothing else around here for miles."

"Fuck, I miss the east coast."

"Why?"

"Much more exciting. You gotta deal with Freebies, too."

"Freebies just get in the way."

Noah sighs quietly next to me as they continue talking. "We have to do something," he whispers.

"Got it," I reply, picking up a chunk of rubble. Before he can stop me, I throw it as hard as I can, as far as I can.

"What the hell?" Person Two says, looking in the direction of the noise. They both emerge from behind the cover where Ava lays, guns held tightly to their chests.

"Let's go. Not like she's going anywhere," Person One, a tall blonde man, says.

"Sure."

They walk cautiously towards where I threw the rock, but just as they are about to disappear from view, two more soldiers appear, carrying a body apiece. I recognize Chris's dark jacket, but I can't tell whether the blood on the floor is his or the other man's.

"Shit, what happened?" Person Two says, returning to his previous post near Ava. Person One follows suit.

One of the new additions answers as he lays the unknown body down. "Somebody whacked Greeves," he pants. "He'll be fine, but he's out cold. Then there's this bastard."

My blood bristles as I realize he's referring to Chris.

"Shit," Noah whispers.

Now there are four conscious soldiers and only two of us. My left arm barely works, and we are weaponless, defenseless. Ava and Chris lay unconscious on the floor next to Greeves.

There is a slight sound behind us, and we freeze.

"I'll look," I offer, knowing Noah won't want to take his eyes off the soldiers.

He nods at me, returning his gaze to our friends. The soldiers seem not to have heard the sound, whatever it was.

I peer over my shoulder to see a little girl in a tattered nightgown. She stands perfectly still in a doorway; her big toe pokes out of one of her shoes, and her hair looks like it hasn't been brushed in months.

She stares at me with striking green eyes and raises one finger silently to her lips. I nod at her.

"Do the rock thing again," Noah whispers, nudging me.

"Are you sure?" I ask, turning back around. Whoever the girl is, she's not important right now.

"Yeah."

I grab a larger chunk of rubble this time, turning it over and over in my hand, trying not to think of how the girl told me to be quiet. I wait for the soldiers to become absorbed in their conversation and then throw it as hard and as far as I can towards the front doors.

They stop dead, turning towards the sound.

"C'mon," Person One says, and they all follow him out of sight.

"Go, go go go," Noah whispers, practically shoving me out from behind our cover. We creep over to Chris and Ava as fast as we can, one eye always in the direction of the soldiers. Just as we reach them, Greeves stirs.

"Clint?" he mumbles, blinking his eyes open. "What...?"

"Shit!" I whisper, wishing I hadn't left my club behind.

"Shh!" Noah says to both me and Greeves. He softens his voice, looking at the man lying on the floor. "Shh. Please."

He and Greeves stare at one another for a moment as I kneel beside Ava. Her chest rises and falls deeply; she looks like she's just sleeping.

"Clint!" Greeves shouts, reaching for his gun.

Noah kicks him hard in the arm, and the following popping sound almost calls my breakfast up.

"Go!" Noah shouts at me, picking Chris up and throwing him over his shoulder. "Run!"

Greeves is screaming as I lift Ava into my arms (she's surprisingly light), and I join him as my shoulder burns with fire. Ignoring the flames the best I can, I run from the lobby and into the hallways. I hear footsteps behind me, more than just Noah's.

I turn sharply to the right. "Go, Noah!"

His footsteps disappear to the left, but at least two pairs continue to follow me, gaining steadily. I push myself faster, doing everything I can to avoid falling over the increasingly prominent rubble.

I stumble, almost losing her. As soon as I recover, I trip again, unable to put a hand out to steady myself. I fall to my knees and look up—I've come to a dead end. They're going to catch us. It's only a matter of seconds.

"Stop!" a male voice shouts, and I can almost hear him unholster his gun. "Don't move!"

I am trembling with fear.

"Who is that?" the voice says. I recognize him as Person Two. "In your arms. Who is she?"

"My friend," I murmur, afraid to turn around. What if they're insane? What if they take us as prisoners? Where are Noah and Chris? Oh, Ankou, what if they're here to bring us back to Carcera?

"Put her down."

"No."

"Put. Her. *Down.*"

The man steps in front of me. I finally look all the way up, past his steely pistol, and into his cold, dead face. Two dark eyes float in his head, absorbing all the light available. His mouth is cruel and hard, hair the color of coal and short as freshly trimmed grass.

The woman standing beside him wears a long red side braid, small curls poking out in odd spots. She is even skinnier than he is but nearly as tall. Her eyes float just like his, a paler blue than the sky.

I shrink my head down again, accepting defeat. I can't win with an unconscious girl and no weapons.

"Do you have any weapons?" the woman asks, and I shake my head. "Answer me verbally. Do you have any weapons?"

"No."

"Wren, go pick her up," the man instructs. The woman steps forward, and I flinch away.

"Don't touch her."

The woman sighs. "We're just going to take the both of you to get medical attention. Let me see that injury on your shoulder."

I stop, allowing her to take Ava from me and inspect my bullet wound without touching it. My whole body shakes in fear as she reaches into her pocket, then whips out a needle and plunges it into my neck.

"Hey!" I shout, falling away from her and putting a hand to my throat. "What *was* that?"

Already my words are slurring, my vision going fuzzy around the edges. I reach a hand toward the wall to steady myself but somehow end up on all fours instead. The woman kneels before me, prepared to catch me when I pass out.

Fighting it is useless, I know, but I can't just give in. What if this drug is killing me, and Ava's dying, too? What if I never see any of my friends again? What if they bring us back to Carcera, to face what we've done? What if—

I WAKE up strapped to a warm bed. Restraints wrap around my ankles and forearms, pressing into my skin so tight I'm going numb. The bright light hurts even from behind my eyelids. My mind feels sluggish and muddled, all my thoughts swirling together in no particular order.

The boys, I think. *I like pancakes. Ava. I want chocolate-chip pancakes. Where am I?*

"Ah, you're awake," a woman says, and I pry one eye open. "Welcome to the Underground." She unbuckles my head strap, allowing me to turn to the side to see her.

She has dark, wavy hair, with gray peeking through at the roots. My mother used to dye her hair to hide the gray—have we been captured? Am I back in Carcera?

Panic sets in. I swallow hard to force down the bile rising in my throat, trying to convince my mind to think linearly. It just won't listen, but somehow, I get the words out.

"Where are my friends? Are they alright?"

"Your friends are fine. They are all recovering from their injuries," she explains in a calm voice. She sounds like my mother, and a knot forms in my throat that I swallow down.

"Chris, the boy with dark hair, he's claustrophobic," I say quickly. "Make sure he isn't tied down; he'll hate that, and—"

She smiles. "I admire how much you care for your companions. I can assure you that he will be fine. Now, you are in the Underground. This tunnel is about four hundred feet below the Surface, one of our deepest here. Long ago, those who survived the attacks escaped into subway tunnels, military bases, and bomb shelters. We have built a society down here, completely independent of Ankou's government. We are a military-based society, which means a lot of things. We focus on getting troops to the Surface for supply raids and assassinations of government officials. Any questions?"

"Attacks?" I gape. "Supply raids? *What?*" My head still hurts.

"A long time ago, the government sent soldiers to kill people in towns that refused to succumb to Borders, at least in this part of the country," she says, reciting it like it's from a textbook. "The east coast remains largely Free, but that doesn't matter much to us. Those who escaped enslavement fled into these tunnels, trying to survive. They built a society fueled by the desire to someday retake their homes on the Surface. Of course, those homes are in ruins now, but the fight continues.

"We need some things that we can't make here, so we send our troops to the Surface for supply raids. We lead raids on agricultural towns for food and livestock in the summer months. The fields are primarily outside the Border, so fresh crops are easy to take in small amounts."

"Lastly, we are attempting to bring down the federal government. We've been trying for years, generations, even. We lead attacks on Border towns and assassinate the officials and soldiers residing there. Then we give the people two options: they can either stay there and build new lives for themselves or come with us. Usually, they pick the latter, but it never ends well for those who choose the first option. Anything else before I let you sit up?"

"Who were those people?"

She sighs. "They were Scouts. We send them to Pevidere about once a month to see if anyone's moved in, or if there are any salvageable supplies. The city looks so bad partly because of us—we use some of the rubble for our construction. The Scouts must've seen you as a threat, and that's why they drugged you and your friends."

"I hit one of them," I admit. "With a chair leg. And my friend, Noah, I think he broke his wrist."

"Ah, so that's what happened to Greeves," she says, nodding. "Well, he'll heal. I'm sure he and others scared the hell out of you, too."

I nod. "How long was I out?" I ask.

"About an hour or so," she replies, unbuckling the straps and letting me sit up. The hospital room sways briefly, but everything stills after a moment or two.

"Now, what is your name, and how did you get here?" she asks, and I sigh, preparing myself for the long story.

I tell her about myself and my family. I tell her about life back in Carcera and about Chris, Ava, and Noah. I tell her the details of our escape and of our time in the woods. I tell her about how we got ambushed in the hospital and of our capture but leave out the part about my family being shot.

"Are you warm?" she asks after a moment of silence. "You're sweating."

"It's not that bad," I say, taken aback at her nonchalance. I was expecting her to be freaked out. "Why?"

"It's only sixty degrees," she says, frowning a bit. "You must be conditioned to the cold. It's a wonder you don't have severe hypothermia."

"We took shelter in caves," I say. "I also had a really good jacket."

She smiles, and I can't help but smile too.

"Can I ask you a question?" I say after a moment of silence. "Two, actually?"

"You just did," she replies. "But yes."

"What's today's date?"

"January ninth, it's a Saturday," she says, checking her watch. "6:06 PM."

"And... why am I here?"

"Because we need you just as much as you need us."

"What?"

"You need us for safety, food, shelter. We need new recruits, if you'll stay," she says, untying the straps around my legs. "You can follow me to your friends."

"Thank you," I say, sliding off the table and trying to ignore how vague her answer was. I grab my muddy and dripping backpack and follow her into a cool white hallway lit only by bluish lights every ten feet. The doors alternate from one side of the hallway to the other. She opens the third door from the corner, gesturing me inside.

Chris and Ava lay in separate hospital beds, hooked up to beeping monitors and one IV each. Noah sits in a metal chair placed right between their beds, holding a hand in each of his own. He stands when he sees me, eyes wide.

Tears of relief and fear spring into my eyes, and Noah knows to hug me immediately. He smells like mud and wet hair, but I don't mind. He is warm and familiar, and that's all that matters right now.

"You okay?" he mumbles into my hair.

"I'm fine," I mutter into his shoulder, sniffling once. "Are you?"

"Same." He pulls away, studying my face and letting a smile tug at the edge of his always-upturned mouth. "We'll be okay."

I echo him. "We'll be okay."

I pull up another chair, and we sit in silence. Noah takes Ava's hand, and I take Chris's, then Noah's. We form a chain, each lending our strength to the others. I lean my head onto Noah's shoulder, feeling a bit nauseous despite my hunger. My limbs are weights, and sleeping for a few days sounds like heaven right about now.

My eyes slide shut only to open again a few moments later when a doctor walks into the room flanked by two nurses.

"Sorry to keep you waiting," he says. His face is narrow, but his blue eyes are soft and kind. "I've had a lot of other patients today." I sit up, neck aching, and unwind my fingers from Noah's.

"You fell asleep about half an hour ago," he whispers to me. I blink a few times in shock; it feels like I closed my eyes for half a minute, not half an hour.

"Thanks," I reply, then address the doctor. "I suppose you want to hear our life stories, too?"

"I'm good," he says kindly, inspecting Ava's head. "I'm Dr. Bisbort, by the way. You are?"

"Katie," I say.

"Noah." He nods to our unconscious friends in turn. "Chris and Ava."

"How did they get hurt?" Dr. Bisbort asks.

"The Scouts drugged them, and we don't know with what," I say. "Something stronger than what we got."

"Ah, makes sense," Dr. Bisbort says. "The Scouts can be a bit heavy-handed, unfortunately. I always advocate sending a medic up there with them, but it never happens. Your friends will be fine. In fact, they look astonishingly good for being out in the elements for... how many days?" he asks, flipping through the charts.

"Good question," Noah says, looking over at me. "What was it, five?"

"Six if you include that first night," I say.

"You're lucky to be here," Dr. Bisbort says, eyes finding the ratty bandages on my shoulder. "Let me take a peek at that arm?"

I tense, taking Noah's hand back in my own. "It's fine, really."

"I won't even touch it if I don't have to," he says, setting down his clipboard. "I'll tell you if I do. There's nothing in my pockets; I'm not like the Scouts."

"Okay," I relent, turning to Noah for reassurance.

"The dressing looks quite good, given the circumstances, but I do need to change it," he says, pulling out some gauze and bandages. "I'm going to get you some painkillers after, too."

"Got it." I nod, gritting my teeth in preparation.

It's obvious that Dr. Bisbort does everything he can to hurry, but the seconds still stretch into hours. I hiss with pain as he cleans the dirt out of the wound, even though it's only a graze. The raw flesh burns as he wipes it with disinfectant like fire is torching my arm.

"It's healing quite well," he comments. "Whoever dressed this took good care of you. And it isn't a deep wound, so there's no nerve damage. You'll regain full mobility very soon."

"Yay," I say flatly, squeezing Noah's hand. He squeezes back.

CHAPTER EIGHT

DR. BISBORT GETS me a sling and some pain meds while giving care instructions. I half-listen, immediately deciding that I won't be using the sling. I don't want anyone to think I'm a target, easy to take down.

"When are they going to wake up?" Noah finally asks, nodding to Ava and Chris.

"Give them a few hours," Dr. Bisbort says. "We can't do much more than let the sedative work its way out of their system. You two go get settled into your dorms—I'll send for someone to show you around. Get some food, get changed, take a shower, then make your way back here." He checks his watch. "Give it three hours or so. Anything else I can do for you guys?"

"How did you find us?" Noah asks.

"Unfortunately, I don't know," Dr. Bisbort sighs. "My guess is that the Scouts were doing a routine sweep of Pevidere and happened upon you guys. We go up there once a month, so, luckily, you got found."

"What connection do you have with Carcera?" I ask, terrified of the answer but needing to know, nonetheless.

"None whatsoever," he says reassuringly. "Carcera is a very protected city. Please understand. They have one of the largest

Borders and some of the strictest laws in the country. We have very opposite ideals here, I assure you. Is that where you came from?"

Noah and I nod.

"Got it. Well, I'm sure this is a lot to process for the both of you. Please try not to explain too much to your friends—they'll be exhausted and probably a little uncomfortable. We'll send someone down in the morning to give them the rundown. Sound good?"

Noah and I nod once more as he stands up and flips open a small phone. "Yeah, can I get Amelia Omenstat down here, Medical Sublevel 8D Floor 3, Room 5? I've got some new recruits down here, and she's next up on the rotation. Thanks. Bye."

He hangs up, then turns back to us. "Amy will be down here in a few minutes. She's a nice girl, amiable. She'll take you up for some food and showers."

"Thank you," I reply.

Noah nods. "Thanks."

Dr. Bisbort smiles as he leaves. "Take care."

Only once the door is closed do I let my composure fade away. "Wow, that hurts."

"You okay?" Noah asks, putting a hand on my good shoulder from behind.

"Noah, if I was okay, would I be saying, 'Wow, that hurts?'" I snap, then instantly regret it. "Sorry."

"Hey." Noah turns me around gently. "We'll be fine, remember? We're always fine."

"Yeah." I nod. "Noah, you don't think that—"

"No," he says quickly, shaking his head. "They don't have anything to do with Carcera. We're okay."

"Okay."

After a minute or two of silence, someone knocks on the door. I open it hesitantly, and a girl with long, dark hair stands on the other side.

"Amelia Omenstat, at your service." She smiles, extending a hand. "My friends just call me Amy."

"Katie Davis," I reply, shaking her hand briefly.

Once the formalities are over with, she turns around, leading us down the hallway. "So, you guys have never been a part of the Underground, amiright?" She speaks like the words trip over her tongue on the way out.

"Yeah," Noah says, glancing over his shoulder one more time at Chris and Ava's room, where we left our backpacks. "Where exactly are we?"

"Well, this is Sublevel 8D, and residential is on Sublevel 8A. You'll be staying up there; it's only a hundred feet below the Surface. Sublevel 8B is shopping and recreation, and Sublevel 8C is training and storage. The size decides levels, and Level 8 is four square miles at the Surface. You could honestly live your whole life without having to leave it."

I shiver, trying not to think about that.

"But," Amy continues, reaching a stairwell and holding the door open for us, then hopping to the front once more. "We leave the Level for funerals, Surface missions, and some holidays. It's not hard to get from Level to Level, but they're pretty far apart, and there are definitely security measures we have to take."

The Border was just another 'security measure' the government had to take.

"The climb up to residential is quite far, so we can take the elevator," Amy says. "Dr. Bisbort gave me a pass to use it for you guys. I'm sure you guys are exhausted from being out in the woods. How did you end up down here?"

"Our friends were drugged," I say. "By the Scouts. We tried to grab them and run, but we got caught. And now we're here."

"Ah," Amy says, pressing the elevator button. "And lemme guess, the Scouts went a little overboard with the sedative?"

"Mhm," Noah says.

"They do that sometimes," Amy says. "I've only been on one mission with them, and we didn't see a soul, but they always had one hand on the needle."

The elevator opens, and she steps inside, beckoning us to follow her. Noah and I have never been in an elevator, but we read about them in Engineering 2. He was always more interested in their mechanics than I was.

Once Amy presses the right button, the elevator closes and shoots upward. Noah and I reach for each other's hands. Amy laughs a little.

"Are you guys dating?" she asks.

My cheeks flush. "No, we're just friends."

"Really good friends," Noah adds, withdrawing his hand to rub the back of his reddening neck. "She likes Chris."

"I do not!" I protest, shoving his arm.

"Yes, you do," he insists, the blush receding from his face. It only makes the dirt and blood stains more apparent.

"You need a shower," I comment, effectively changing the subject.

"Have you seen your hair?" he jokes. "You need to wash that, like, *now.*"

"Rude!" Amy laughs. Her effortless joy is so different that it's almost confusing. "Never tell a girl she needs to wash her hair. Actually, I think frozen hair is a good look for you, Katie."

"Thank you," I say. "Uh, where exactly can I get a shower?"

"You guys can come back to the room I share with my girlfriend, Sam," she says. "Noah, you can shower in the room down the hall; it's an empty one that we use when newbies come in. I think there are still some clothes in there, too."

"Cool," Noah says as the elevator comes to a stop. We disembark, and Amy leads us down another two hallways. Teenagers and young adults stare as we walk past; I can't even imagine how horrible we must look.

Noah waves at a young man, who sneers at us and whispers something to the girl standing next to him. Noah raises his eyebrows, looking back at me in annoyance. I roll my eyes, leaning around him to wave at some people with false sweetness. They scoff, all turning to their friends.

"Ignore them," Amy says, loudly enough for them to hear. "They're not worth your time. All Ignavus, if you ask me."

The people sigh huffily, rolling their eyes and retreating into their dorms like rabbits into a hole. I keep one eye on the hallway behind us as Amy knocks on one of the doors.

"Sam," she says, opening the door and walking inside. "I was next on the newbie rotation. Meet Noah and Katie."

A girl with curly blonde hair steps out of the bathroom, clad in nothing but a sports bra and a pair of athletic shorts. Noah and I snap our eyes away, giving her as much privacy as we can when standing in the doorway of her home.

"Amy, you could've told me there was a guy," Sam grumbles, throwing a t-shirt over her head. "You can turn around now. I don't bite."

Noah and I slowly turn to face her, locking eyes for a moment as we do so. His gaze screams, *'Help! Pretty girl! Not Ava!'* It's kind of funny, to be honest.

Amy gestures to us. "Their other two friends are in the infirmary, recovering from the Scouts' sedative."

"Were your friends feisty, or were the Scouts a little overdramatic?" Sam asks, bending over to pull her hair into a high ponytail.

"Probably a bit of both," I admit.

"They definitely put up a fight," Noah adds. "I mean, Katie clubbed someone with a chair leg."

I shove him. "I'm pretty sure you bit him."

Sam laughs dryly. "Oh, good, you'll fit right in. Katie, you can shower in here; you'll fit in some of our clothes for the time being. Noah, there's a spare room down the hall if you want to use that. The clothes in there should fit you." Her voice cracks slightly, but I wonder if that's just what she always sounds like.

Amy rifles through a drawer in the dresser, pulling out a pair of black leggings and a white t-shirt. "These should fit you, Katie. No offense, but you kind of reek. Go shower."

"Thanks," I say, nodding once at Noah.

He nods back, and Sam leads him through the door. I step into the bathroom and stop dead when I glimpse my reflection in the mirror. My hair is damp from the ice melting, and my clothes are wrinkled and covered in mud. I have scratches on my face and hands and dirt under my fingernails. No wonder the people in the hallway stared at me—I look like death frozen over.

Without looking at myself again, I turn the water on and fully undress for the first time in over a week.

I've never had a better shower. My arm burns slightly, but the gauze is waterproof, and Dr. Bisbort's painkillers are setting in. The water pressure is fantastic, the shampoo smells like apples, and the clothes are clean and dry. I feel bare in them, like too much of my body is visible even though it's covered. I'll have to ask Sam or Amy for a jacket later.

When I step out of the bathroom with my hair in a tight braid, Sam is the one waiting for me.

"Amy volunteered to take Noah to the dining hall," she explains. "He looked pretty hungry. I'll take you down there."

"Thanks," I say, looking down at the wad of filthy clothes in my hands. "What should I do with these?"

Sam wrinkles her nose. "Unless you have a ridiculous sentimental attachment to them, I would get rid of them."

"Okay," I reply, tossing them in the trash can, knowing I should be sad but completely unable to feel any remorse. My once-favorite sweater is at the bottom of the list of things I need to mourn. "Shoes?"

"Those go, too," she says, standing up and opening the closet door. She digs around the bottom for a moment, then comes back up. "Size seven and a half?"

"How'd you know?"

"Lucky guess." She stands up and hands me a pair of black sneakers with orange laces. "The Head Trainer will get you guys all squared away in dorms tomorrow. For tonight, you and Noah can stay here."

"Oh, okay," I say, tugging on a pair of socks and then the sneakers. The thought of spending the night away from Chris and Ava is enough to send me into a mild panic.

"Or you could spend the night in the infirmary with your friends," she offers. "Trust me. I know what it's like."

"Thank you." I smile, following her through the door. I was raised to ignore my curiosity. It doesn't always work, but I try anyway.

We walk in silence for a bit, winding through the hallways until we come to a stairwell. Sam begins the descent, taking the stairs two at a time. I only go one at a time; the stairs seem so narrow compared to the wide ones back home.

"How long were you out there?" she asks.

"Six days," I say.

"Was it cold?"

"Think of the coldest place you've ever been, and then make it colder."

"Ouch. How'd you get shot?"

Her question takes me back to the night of our escape and all the terror of those hours. Sprinting for our lives through the darkness, the pain of being shot... my brother's death. I shudder.

"The guards tried to catch us the night we escaped," I say, not wanting to go much further.

"What happened to your family?"

"They're probably dead." My bluntness shocks even me; I've been spending too much time with Noah.

"Sorry to hear." Sympathy edges into her voice, but not enough to make me think she pities me. I'm thankful for that.

"Me, too."

At this point, we come to a door in the stairwell that she leads me through. The dining hall is two times the size of our cafeteria back at school, with a ceiling so high that it feels like being under a starless sky.

The food is served buffet-style, and everyone stares at us as we make our plates. I don't even know half of the food, so I take what looks familiar.

"Sorry," Sam whispers to me as we grab water bottles from a fridge. "Everyone knows everyone around here. We don't get people straight from the Surface often."

"What time is it?" I ask as we make our way over to Amy and Noah, who are inhaling food by the pound.

"About 7:50," Sam replies, checking her black watch. "Curfew is at 8:30, so we've got time."

"Why are you eating such plain food?" Amy asks, observing my plate of raw veggies, chicken breast, a buttered roll, and an apple.

"This isn't plain," I retort, feeling slightly defensive over the food I've grown up with.

"Yeah, it is," Sam replies, raising one sculpted eyebrow. How is it so perfect? It's like it's stenciled onto her face.

"Is there a certain time we have to be awake in the morning?" Noah asks between mouthfuls, trying to change the subject.

"It doesn't matter for you guys yet," Amy says. "You haven't started training. Once you start, you *have* to be up by six. Of course, Wakeup will wake you up tomorrow anyway, that's the point, but you can just chill for the day. I'm sure the Head Trainer will summon you to his office at some point."

"Wow," I say, taking another bite of my apple. The full force of my hunger is finally hitting, and I'm chewing too fast to speak much. "Training?"

"You guys will probably meet with the Head Trainer tomorrow and be assigned to your squad," Amy explains.

"If you're staying, of course," Sam interjects.

Amy nods. "Right. If you do choose to stay, you'll be assigned your squad and start training the next day, unless you're really hurt or sick. You two would be fine, but your friends—"

"They're fine," Noah says sharply, then winces as he realizes the bite in his voice. "Actually, we should probably be getting back. Sound good, Katie?"

I stand up to go instead of answering him, still chewing the last bite of my apple.

SAM AND AMY drop us off at the hospital. Amy scribbles their phone number on a piece of paper and tells us to call if we need anything.

Chris and Ava are still unconscious. I sigh heavily, sitting on the edge of Chris's bed and brushing some untamed hair away from his eyes.

"He'll be fine," Noah says.

"Dr. Bisbort said a couple of hours. It's been a couple of hours."

"Katie." Noah stands next to me, taking my hand in his own. I do not know whether he's lending me strength or I'm giving it to him. "It's Chris and Ava. They're always fine, remember?"

"Damn right," Chris mutters.

My heart leaps into my throat as I whirl around to look at him. He still looks pale, dirty, and exhausted, but he's alive. He's okay.

"You heard all that?" Noah asks, punching him lightly in the arm.

"Every word," he says, cracking his eyes open.

"Nice to see you," I say, voice choked. Oh, Ankou, he's *okay*.

"I exist, too," Ava says from her bed, lifting her head up briefly. Noah practically launches himself over to her, clasping her nearest hand in both of his.

Chris smiles a little. "You look awfully clean."

"Long story," I say. "You tired?"

"Exhausted," he replies. "Which is weird, considering I've been unconscious for... how long?"

"Good question," I say. "Four, five hours, maybe."

"Damn. Where are we?"

"That's a long story, too."

"You tired?"

"You ask a lot of questions," I tease.

"C'mere," he says, opening his arms wide and inviting me to lay next to him. I oblige, my heart beating out of my ribcage. He is warm and solid, so *there* that it's nearly impossible not to fall asleep immediately. I look over to find that Noah has curled himself around Ava, both already sound asleep.

"Katie?" Chris whispers.

"Yeah?" I reply, exhaling slowly. I can feel his heartbeat under my ear.

"Why is your heart beating so fast?"

"So many questions," I mumble, already drifting into sleep. "I'll tell you tomorrow."

CHAPTER NINE

CHRIS IS GONE when I wake up. The bed feels cold without his warmth, although the covers are pulled high around my shoulders.

The missing boy pokes his head out of the bathroom. "Morning." His hair is flat on one side and wild on the other, a bit of toothpaste dotting the corner of his mouth.

"Hey." I yawn, pushing the covers off. "Sleep well?"

"Better than I have in way too long," he replies. "You?"

I groan and stretch. "Fantastic. Where are Ava and Noah?"

"A doctor came in this morning and explained everything," Chris says, running a hand through his hair. He looks so small in the over-sized hoodie he's wearing—my heart jumps at the sight.

"He had room numbers for the four of us. Ava went for a shower, and Noah went with her. I think he's working on breakfast."

"So, you know everything?"

"Yeah. Military society hellbent on fighting the central government for the power of the Surface."

"Yeah. Guess we should wait for the others to talk about this, right?"

"Probably for the best."

"You completely overwhelmed by it?"

"Yep. You?"

"Oh, absolutely." I shiver as my bare feet hit the tile floor. "Nice hoodie."

"Thanks," he says, looking down and pulling at the fabric. "It's huge —you could probably fit in here with me."

"You think so?" I ask, standing in front of him. I didn't realize how sizable the height difference between us is, and I never noticed that little freckle on his neck.

The toothpaste on the corner of his lip is infuriating—is it wrong to want to stand on my toes and kiss it? I'm pretty sure that's a strange thought to have about my best friend. I shouldn't want to kiss him; he's like my brother.

But he isn't, not really. I never felt this way about Lucas. Of course, I didn't, because he was *actually* my brother. Chris is just a best friend with the honorary title of 'brother.'

I settle for wiping the toothpaste away with my thumb, resolved to think about what my pounding heart means later.

OUR NEW HOMES are in Cirro Hall, which is shockingly easy to find. We shower, unpack whatever belongings we have left, and resolve ourselves to yet another difficult discussion.

I sit down on one of the twin-sized beds in the boy's room. These rooms are small and cramped; each has a fake window painted on the wall, complete with trees and a mountain. This one even has a sunset.

"What do we do?" I say.

"I think we should stay," Ava says. "I mean, they saved our lives."

"I agree," Chris says. "They've been kind to us so far. They would've hurt us by now if they wanted to."

"Ava, they're the ones who almost killed us in the first place," Noah argues, leaning against the low dresser. "And we would have to join the military."

"I would be fine with that," I offer.

"Well, of course, you would be okay with that, Katie," Chris sighs.

"I just want to fight back," I say, folding my arms over my chest despite the stiffness in my left shoulder.

"Yeah," Noah says. "Same here. Still, I'm not sure about killing people."

"Same," Chris says. "But it doesn't look like we have any other options."

"What about escaping?" Noah suggests.

"We don't know how to get out of here, and we would die out there," Ava says. "We almost did."

"Because of them, Ava," Noah says, a hint of exasperation in his voice. "They're the ones that drugged you and Chris into oblivion."

"Hey, I needed that nap," she retorts, trying to lighten the mood. "They saved us. I don't think we can argue that."

"Agreed," Chris says. "And the fact that she's not in trouble for clubbing someone over the head says a lot." He nods to me.

"True," I say. "I should be in deep shit for that."

"What if you are and just don't know it yet?" Noah asks.

"I told the woman in the hospital who was there when I woke up. She didn't seem to mind."

He is silent for a moment—a rarity. "I don't think we know enough to make a good decision," he finally says.

"Fair enough," I say, trying to keep the peace. "We'll just watch our backs." Chris's eyes find mine. They're soft and warm, a comforting blue that calms my nerves.

"Time to get ready," Ava says, clearing her throat. "We have a full afternoon of getting lost ahead of us."

"Are we going back to our room?" I say, cheeks hot.

She stands and stretches, laughing preemptively at her own joke. "Yeah, I wanna unpack a bit."

"We'll meet you guys in an hour?" Noah suggests.

"Sounds good," I say.

"See you later," Chris says, putting a hand on my lower back to guide me through the door.

"See you then," I say quietly, looking up at him. He stares at me for a moment, then bends down so slow it's painful and kisses my cheek.

My cheeks flush even redder, eyes widening with elated shock as he pulls away, rubbing the back of his neck sheepishly.

"Shoot me," Noah grumbles playfully, opening the door to guide us out.

"As someone who's been shot, I don't recommend it," I tease, slipping through the door and grinning at Ava once we're in the safety of the hallway.

She says nothing, just bumps me with her elbow, and raises her eyebrows. Despite everything, I can't help but grin.

———

"As official residents, the four of you are required to fill out funeral paperwork," the woman says. She hands us each a clipboard with a few sheets of paper. We are seated in the Head Trainer's office, and his secretary is in charge of meeting with us first.

"As you already know, the Underground is a military-based society," she says. "To cut the cost and time of funerals, we cremate each of our deceased soldiers individually. The ashes are then mixed with firework powder, which will be set off at a ceremony after each mission to the Surface with more than ten casualties. Page one explains this, while page two is where you fill out basic information about yourself. It includes your current place of residence, relatives and/or friends, and birthday. Please also specify what type of firework is preferable for you—that's on page three."

"Ma'am, we don't know our actual birthdates," Chris says. "We were told that we all share a communal one."

"You can write that down if that's all you know," she says. "The Head Trainer should be here in just a minute."

She exits the office, leaving us to read about what a firework is.

Chris finishes the informational page first. "No way." He tosses his clipboard onto the small glass coffee table with a bang. "I'm not doing this."

"We have no other choice," I say. "This is the way they do funerals here."

"I'm not going to be an explosion," he says stubbornly. "*Anything* but that. That's too... no."

"It's how it is," Noah says. "We don't have another option."

"Could we explain the situation to the Head Trainer?" Ava suggests. "Maybe he'll let it slide, considering the circumstances."

I know that's not going to happen, and I think they know it, too.

The form is a bit odd. I write down my address (221 Cirro Hall), my friends' names, and then the part about what firework I would like to be. I pick a gold one.

Almost immediately after I am done filling out my form, the Head Trainer enters the room. He is built like a mountain, tall and solid, with close-cropped hair and a mouth that naturally turns down.

"Hello," he says, voice powerful but not unkind. "My name is Arthur, and I am the Head Trainer here in Level 8 of the Underground. That means I oversee all training, organize missions, and take charge of funeral arrangements. I also put new residents into their squads. What are your names?"

"I'm Noah," Noah says.

"Ava."

"Chris."

"And I'm Katie."

"Very well," he says. "I assume you would all like to be a part of the same squad?" We nod. "Alright."

He sits down at his desk and rifles through a filing cabinet. "Each squad has a maximum of ten soldiers, and the trainers are not included in that count. You must train for at least two months before we grant you the privilege of going to the Surface. Even if you do go to the Surface, you must continue your training. Curfew is at 8:30, Lights-out at 10:00, and Wakeup at 6:00. Breakfast for the soldiers is served from 6:15 to 6:45, and you must report to your training area no later than 7:00. Your trainer will tell you what training area to report to the night before. Lunch is served from 11:00 to 1:00, and training ends at 5:30. Half of your day is classroom studies, while the other half is physical training, and you have Sundays off. Any questions?"

"Do we have the option of leaving?" Noah asks, and Arthur nods.

"You can leave if you wish, and we won't take any offense to that. But personally speaking, I highly advise against it. There's no room in this world for a third party. You either fight with us or try to join a new Border town, which has never been done before. The guards will execute you before you even make it to the gates. And in theory, you could head east, but I don't think you'd fit in very well."

"We'll stay," I say quickly, ignoring the concept of going east. "And can we choose what kind of squad we're in?"

"You'll be trained as regular combat for at least a year. After that, you can transfer to any number of different squads if you pass the transfer test. It will be up to your trainer to advise you and help you with that."

"What's the exam like?" Chris asks, already thinking one step ahead.

"Each field has a physical and mental test that must be passed to be placed into a new squad. Some are more of a written exam, while others are tests of strength. If you four are very close, I suggest all transferring to the same field, as your dorms would also be reassigned. Any more questions?"

We all glance at each other, but no one speaks up.

"You will be assigned to Squad 5609," Arthur continues. "Your trainer is Cecilia Adder, and there are two other soldiers in your squad—Samantha Sinderfield and Amelia Omenstat, whom you may have already met. Training starts tomorrow."

"Thank you, sir," Chris says, and we head back to our rooms to prepare for our new future.

"I DON'T KNOW how much I like this," Noah says once we get back to our room. "I don't want to be a soldier."

"Me neither," Chris says.

"It doesn't look like we have a choice," I say. "If we're going to live here, this is how it will be. We have time to train before going to the Surface."

"Well, curfew is in..." Noah checks his watch. "Three hours, thirty-six minutes, and four seconds. We should go do something before then, take our minds off this for a little while. It's been too long since we've gotten to relax."

"This girl gave me directions to the Activity Center," Ava says, taking a piece of wrinkled paper out of her nightstand drawer. "Down three flights of the nearest stairwell, turn right, take the second left, down one flight, turn left, take the third left, and it's the first right. Big open hall with side areas."

"Let's go," Noah says, grabbing his room key off the dresser.

Thanks to Ava's surprisingly helpful directions, it doesn't take long to get to the Activity Center. Brightly lit vendors line the walls of the open cavern, offering any sort of game imaginable.

"Woah," Noah says, eyes wide.

"Woah is right," Ava says. "Look, they have a dance game."

She points to a vendor with two rubber pads on the floor and a large screen in front of it. Two girls move their feet according to the pattern the screen tells them, laughing as they throw in arm and leg movements. Strange noises come from the screen, with a rhythm they dance to.

"Come *on*." She tugs on my arm. I roll my eyes but smile anyway, following her to the dance game.

"Do we have to pay?" Ava asks the guy standing next to the machine.

"All free," he says, flashing her a grin. He pushes stringy dark hair away to reveal a silver piece of metal in his eyebrow.

Noah puts a hand on Ava's shoulder in a way that can only be described as protective. She smiles back at the man regardless, and the other two girls step off their platforms. Ava takes my hand, pulling me onto one and positioning herself on the other.

The guy presses a few buttons on a smaller screen. "You guys new?"

"Got here yesterday," Ava says.

"You ever hear music?" the guy asks, and we shake our heads. "Figures. Just dance to the beat and have fun. I'm Anthony, by the way."

"Ava," she says, giving him another quick smile. I stay quiet.

The rhythm starts again when he presses the button, and Ava begins dancing right away. She follows all the steps on the screen but adds her own Ava-ness to it, too. Noah's eyes are filled with something akin to pride. It dawns on me that he's never seen her dance before, except on the river. I shiver at the thought of freezing water and the ice giving way beneath his feet.

It takes Anthony's expression of adoration to bring me back to reality. His gaze matches Noah's, and a twinge of anger pinches in my stomach.

"Nicely done," Anthony says as the following two people step onto the platforms after Ava's finished. He starts the music for them, then steps over to us. "What squad are you in? Or have you not been assigned yet?"

"5609," Noah says, wrapping an arm around Ava's shoulders. "We start training tomorrow."

"Ah, the great Cecilia Adder," Anthony says. "What a hardass. I heard she lost her husband a year ago or something.'"

"What squad are you in?" Ava asks, obviously the only one of us taking pleasure in this conversation.

"5547," he says. "Communications, mainly. You guys are front-line combat. Suicidal maniacs if you ask me. Always gotta be heroes."

"What do you mean?"

"I'm just saying, combat squads, think they're invincible. You guys are flesh and blood just like the rest of us, even if you are an Avenda."

"Yeah, I'm pretty sure we know that," I say, gesturing to the wad of gauze on my arm.

"Just saying." He turns to Ava. "I'll see you later? I'm having some friends over, Cedar Hall."

"Don't count on it."

"Why not?"

"I'll probably be busy." She pointedly takes Noah's hand, leading him and the rest of us away.

We end up back in our room, where Chris begins the lecture we all knew was coming. After several minutes of ranting about "keeping the peace," "staying safe," and "keeping our heads down," Noah finally gets his say.

"Chris, that guy was an ass, and you know it."

"But we have to be a part of this unit, or they could kick us out."

"Well, he can't call us suicidal maniacs when we haven't even started training yet," Ava says.

"Still," Chris says. "Just because we have freedom doesn't mean we can do whatever we want. Rules exist down here too, you know."

"Yeah. One of them goes something like, 'don't label people as suicidal maniacs when they've been here for two days.'"

"Oh, Ankou, cut it out," I finally say. "We are up each other's butts right now. Why don't we all take some time to ourselves to think about things? Get out of each other's hair for a bit."

Ava and Chris oblige without hesitation, ducking into the hallway with nothing more than a wave, but Noah sticks around.

"Well, what do you think I should've said?" he asks the instant the door closes.

"Tell her to stop," I scoff, leaning back against the doorframe. In my heart, I know today wasn't her fault, but she shouldn't have been flirting with some guy she doesn't know and then implying that she was with Noah. We still don't know who to trust besides ourselves, and he could've been dangerous.

"So now this is her fault?" Noah always asks questions during an argument; I don't really know why.

"I'm not saying this—"

"But you are."

"No, I'm not!" I snap, standing up straight again. "Noah, if you would listen to me for half a second—"

"I'm listening."

I take a deep breath, trying to collect myself. I fail.

"They could've left us up there to die!" I shout. "They had every reason to leave us for dead, and they *didn't*!"

"So we're supposed to give up our lives for their endless crusade?"

he spits, uncrossing his arms. "This doesn't mean anything, Katie!" He sweeps an arm around the room. "We're just bodies to them!"

"Of course, we aren't!" I yell. "We're people. All of us are *people!* Maybe you'd understand if you weren't too blind to see that."

"So now I'm stupid?"

"For not seeing what's right in front of your face, yeah, you are."

He recoils as if struck, and I know I've pushed the wrong button. I should never have called him stupid; that's one of the only things on Noah's out-of-bound list.

He sets his jaw, eyes going cold once more. "We should've left you up there and saved ourselves from your mess."

I slam the door on the way out.

I END up at a hair salon only an hour before curfew, hungry and tired yet determined to stay out for as long as possible.

"Hi, can I help you?" a young woman says from behind the front desk.

The salon is dimly lit, with abstract artwork lining the black walls. Several women are getting their haircuts at chairs along the edge of the room.

"Can I, uh, get my hair cut?" I say stupidly, distracted by the strangeness of the place. "Short, please."

"How short?"

"Um, about here." I raise a hand to the bottom of my ear.

"Yeah, right this way," she says, leading me to the back of the salon to the sinks.

A woman with long lavender hair and thick black glasses steps out from behind the sinks to introduce herself.

Before I know it, a pile of my hair sits on the floor beneath my feet. The clippers are warm against my neck, and I'm almost too scared to look in the mirror. Almost.

"KATIE?" Chris calls from the bathroom of my room when I finally get back. I don't know why he's in here—maybe Ava will stay with Noah tonight, and they can work out whatever they're dealing with. I'll stay on my side of the wall, though. "Is that you?"

"Yeah, it's me," I say, shutting the door behind me. I take a deep breath and glance in the mirror. My hair sweeps across my forehead and stops just below my ears. I look like a tougher version of myself—I like it.

"Ava and Noah are talking to the kids across the hall, actually making friends. I was going to—" He stops short when he sees my hair. "Woah."

"Like it?" I smile, standing up and clasping my hands together in front of my chest. "I decided that with it being so long, it would—"

He exhales the next words. "You look beautiful."

"Well, thanks, I mean..." I trail off, raising an eyebrow.

"Did I... oh, Ankou," he says, eyes wide. "Really, I just mean—"

"Don't explain," I say quickly. "You'll only make it worse for yourself."

He laughs. "You're right. But hey, how 'bout a little warning before you go do something like that?" He rubs the back of his neck with one hand as his cheeks light up red. "I mean, you just stormed off, and none of us knew where you were. I mean, what if you got lost? You could get in a lot of trouble. And really, it's not smart for us to be alone around here. We don't know anyone, and—"

"You're rambling," I say, making him blush harder.

"I am not!"

"I can feel your cheeks getting hotter from here," I say, and he looks away, biting back a smile.

"I hate you," he jokes, looking back up at me.

"I hate you, too." I smile, brushing past him into the bathroom.

"KATIE, WAKE UP," Ava says, shaking my shoulder.

"No," I mumble, rolling over and pulling the blanket over my head. "I slept for four hours, leave me alone."

The blanket is ripped off me, and I gasp at the shock of cold air. "Hey!"

"We start training today," Ava says, flicking the light switch and forcing me to shield my eyes. "Up."

"Fine," I grumble, rolling out of bed and wincing as my bare feet hit the cold floor. "I'm up. Happy now?"

"Very much so." She smiles, walking into the bathroom to get ready. I sigh, run a hand through my newly cut hair, and walk over to our closet.

For my first day, I pick out a plain white t-shirt and black shorts. I run a comb through my hair while I wait for Ava to get out of the bathroom, marveling at how easy it is. No more knots, tangles, or lumpy ponytails.

"Finally. It only took you forever," I tease as Ava walks out of the bathroom, eyes alert and hair in a fresh ballet bun.

"Still gotta look good, right?" she jokes, shoving my arm playfully. Apparently, we're fine now, even though we went to bed last night in silence. I barely slept, plagued by nightmares.

"Right." I roll my eyes jokingly, turning on the water to wash my face.

When we're done, we meet the boys in their room, then the four of us head down to breakfast. I have a piece of toast, some grapes, and a handful of almonds.

"These waffles are beautiful," Ava says, drowning yet another in syrup.

"Careful how much you eat; you'll get sick later," Chris warns, but she shrugs him off.

"Sick, schmick. I never throw up."

"Famous last words," Noah jokes, and Ava rolls her eyes at him.

A HALF-HOUR LATER, we're standing at the start of the two-mile track, and Ava isn't the only one who looks queasy. Our trainer, Cecilia, wastes no time getting to know us.

"Soldier!" she yells, standing directly in front of Noah. She has to look up at him because she is only my height. "What is your name?"

"Noah Grim," he says quietly. Even though he towers over her, he flinches away.

"That's Noah Grim, *ma'am!*" she yells. After a moment of silence, she raises an eyebrow, inviting him to repeat it.

After yet another moment, he realizes what she wants. "Noah Grim, ma'am."

"Where are you from?"

"Carcera, ma'am."

"What is your reason for training?"

"I... well..." he falters.

Her black eyes shine. "*Tell me!*"

"This is where I was assigned, ma'am," he says timidly.

Cecilia moves on to me next. "You soldier!" She stands only inches from my face. I stare ahead, looking at the way her close-cropped hairline runs along her dark skin in a perfectly straight line. "What is your name?"

"Kaitlyn Davis, ma'am!" I yell back.

"What is your reason for being here?"

"I wish to serve this military, ma'am!" Does it count as a lie if you aren't sure if you mean it?

"Good answer," she mutters, turning away. She yells at Chris next, and then Ava, who is the only one of us who seems completely unfazed.

"Alright, now that that's out of the way, we can start training," she says, pacing in front of the six of us. "Today, we will begin with a two-mile run. You have twenty minutes. Go!" She steps out of the way as Amy and Sam begin running, pulling out a stopwatch and clicking it. Ava, Chris, Noah, and I all pause for a second, but we follow anyway. For all we know, disagreeing could be dangerous.

CHAPTER TEN

"Because you'll be spending up to ten hours a day together, you need to learn how to work as a team." We've arrived at the end of our run with Cecilia waiting for us. I glance at Sam and Amy—they barely broke a sweat. The rest of us are gasping for air.

"Form One is simple. The six of you will move as one body to complete a set of movements uniformly. Sinderfield and Omenstat, you'll teach everyone the steps. Work together for an hour and a half or so, then show me."

Most of us have regained our composure as we gather around Sam in a loose circle.

"Listen up. The moves are simple, but it's working as a team that matters. Every pause must last the same amount of time. Every movement must have the same height and force. I can take the girls—Amy, you take the boys. We'll teach you the movements, then put it all together."

We do as we're told, running through the movements separately before putting them together. Ava puts an extra flourish on it that Sam has to tell her not to do, and apparently, my posture isn't straight enough. Sam threatens to tie a pole to my back once or twice.

Eventually, the three of us get it down without a hitch, and then we bring the boys into the picture.

"Noah, shorter steps," Amy comments.

"I have long legs!"

"And we're short. Adjust."

We wait until the very end of our hour and a half to show Cecilia. If she is impressed, she doesn't show it.

***

"Davis, stay with me," Cecilia says. "The rest of you, go for another quarter mile."

They take off while I stand with her. "Yes, ma'am?"

"Have you ever received any physical training before? Aside from school sports."

"No, ma'am."

"You lived in Carcera all your life?"

"Until about two weeks ago, yes, ma'am."

"Okay. And how long have you known the other three?"

"About twelve years now. We've grown up together."

She nods. "I see. Well, is there anything I should know about you, in particular?"

I rack my brain for something. "I..."

"Spit it out, Davis. I got three more of these to do."

"Our families... our families are all dead. All of them."

Her face darkens for a moment as if a cloud were passing overhead. Oh, Ankou, I miss being outside.

"Very well then. Thank you. When they come back, tell Castellano to come chat with me. The rest of you are rerunning the same distance."

"SHE HATES US." I sigh, stumbling up the stairs nine hours later. "Absolutely *hates* us."

"Yes, she does," Ava mutters.

"We could go to the Head Trainer and ask him to switch us to another squad," Chris suggests. At that moment, Sam and Amy arrive behind us.

"He'll never let you." Sam wipes her sweaty forehead with a towel.

Amy sends us an encouraging smile. "You guys did pretty good today, anyway."

"Well, we feel the opposite," Ava grumbles.

"Waffles for breakfast?" Sam asks, and Ava nods. "What I thought."

"Be grateful you guys did well with the introductions," Amy says. "On our first day, there was a girl who *cried*. Cecilia made her run an extra mile."

"Really?" Chris asks, eyes wide.

"Yeah!" Amy says. Her eyes light up, but it looks forced like she's sad but can't show it.

"Wow," I say. "Who is she?"

Amy glances at Sam, who begins to answer. "Well." She pauses, rubbing the back of her neck with one hand. "Her name was Sasha Marse. She died on our last mission on the Surface."

"I'm sorry," I say quickly. "I didn't mean to—"

"No, it's fine," Sam says. "Nothing wrong with asking."

"We didn't see it," Amy adds. "All I know is that she saved us when I was shot."

"You were shot?" Chris says, then thinks better of showing his curiosity. "Sorry. I don't mean to pry."

"God, who raised you people, nuns?" Sam jokes and, seeing our confusion, sighs. "Never mind."

"I was shot in my right shoulder, clean through," Amy continues. "Got knocked out when I went down, woke up in a field hospital two days later."

"Meanwhile, I lived off black coffee and didn't sleep a wink." Sam elbows Amy jokingly.

"Hey, it's not my fault you didn't sleep!" Amy smiles, nudging her in retaliation. "It's not like I got shot *on purpose*."

"Yes, you did." Sam grins, turning to us. "You guys have any battle stories?"

"Katie was shot," Chris says.

"Just a graze," I interject. "It's nothing, really."

"She got shot when we were escaping our town," Noah says. "Chris almost had to carry her through the woods to get here."

I shove him on the arm playfully. "It was a scratch. Seriously. Barely warrants a band-aid anymore."

At this point, we arrive on our floor. Sam and Amy depart for their room in Nimbo Hall.

I win the rock-paper-scissor game for showers and walk out of the bathroom twenty minutes later, exhausted and starving. Ava practically leaps into the bathroom after asking me to go get her a bowl of plain rice, veggie strips, and some packets of soy sauce.

"I don't like the pre-made stir-fry," she says moodily, wrinkling her nose. "Too sticky."

I roll my eyes but head down to the dining hall with Noah to make her homemade stir fry all the same, agreeing to meet her in the boys' room after. I have to walk twice as fast as him just to keep up with his long legs.

"She's mad, you know." Noah breaks the silence as we descend the stairs two at a time.

"Why?"

"She feels like she's been hit by a bus." He jumps the last three steps to the landing. I jump from the fourth, not to be outdone.

"Her feet hurt?" I say, and he nods. "Well, I think we all feel that way."

"Just warning you, she'll be complaining when we get back."

WE MAKE it the rest of the trip without speaking again, but the silence doesn't last long.

"I don't want to do this anymore," Ava says as soon as she opens the door to the boys' room.

Noah leans over to whisper, "Told you."

"There is no way I am doing that again tomorrow," Ava continues, and I elbow past her.

I set my tray down on the dresser and hand her the bowl of ingredients. "A thank-you would be nice, maybe."

"What's going on?" Chris mumbles, rubbing one eye as he steps out of the bathroom clad only in sweatpants. I look away hastily, busying myself with taking the food off the trays.

Noah whistles and Ava rolls her eyes.

Chris quickly throws a hoodie over his head. "Sorry, I left this out here."

"Damn, son. Showin' off for the girls?" Noah throws an arm around his shoulders.

"Ew, gross," Chris says, ducking out from under him. "Well, not ew, I mean, I..." He trails off.

"This is why I should've never followed you people into that Ankou-forsaken hospital," Ava huffs.

"This isn't my fault!" I say.

"Are you saying it was mine?"

"Ava, you're the one who wanted to research your uncle. You're the one who bolted."

"You did that with me! You *agreed*." Her voice cracks on the last word, but her dark eyes are still on fire.

"I didn't agree to run into the woods in January and then effectively get kidnapped by an underground military society. I didn't sign up for this, and they sure as hell didn't either." I gesture to the boys, who have been slowly inching back towards the wall.

"Hey, we aren't a part of this," Noah says quickly, raising his hands in surrender.

Ava and I both roll our eyes, turning back to one another.

"None of us signed up for this," I continue. "And it sucks, big time. Losing our families is hard. Training is *hard*."

"Yeah, if the first day was hard, imagine what *forever* will be like."

"The first day's always the hardest."

"Well, it looks like we'll get to test that theory daily for the *rest of our lives!*"

"ENOUGH!" Noah yells, stepping between us. "Katie, you're spending the night in here. I'll stay with Ava in the other room. You're both wrong; now leave each other alone."

We all nod, wide-eyed and slightly terrified.

Noah picks up the tray with his stuff and stalks out the door without another word, Ava on his heels. Once the door closes behind them, I sigh.

Chris turns to face me. "That was uncalled for."

"*What* was uncalled for?"

"That entire fight," he says. "It's not her fault what happened. It's not anyone's fault. And you said it yourself. You committed a crime, too."

"That doesn't mean I would've run if they came to my house first."

"But you ran anyways."

"Yeah, no shit. You showed up at my door saying I'd be killed. It was run or die."

"That's what Ava thought, too."

"No, Chris—" I stop myself short, take a deep breath, and continue. "I wouldn't have run if they came to me first."

"Can you say that for sure?"

"*Yes.* Ankou, yes. I never... I never would've left him if they didn't have guns drawn, if you weren't already going." My throat aches. "I have to go. I'll be back later."

With that, I turn and leave, unsure where I will go. He doesn't follow me, but I find myself wishing he did.

I END up in Nimbo Hall, wishing I knew Sam and Amy's address. Deciding I have no other option but to ask someone, I knock on a random door.

A girl with dark hair opens it. "Yeah?"

"Do you know where I can find Sam and Amy? I heard they live in this hall," I say. "They're my squad members."

"You an Avenda?" The girl asks, looking me up and down with hawk-like eyes. I lean away, self-consciously crossing my arms over my chest.

"I don't know," I reply. "My name's Katie. I'm new."

"Antoinette Latrodectus," she says, sticking out a hand. I shake it cautiously; her nails dig into my wrist. "They're two doors down, same side."

"Thanks," I say, walking away briskly.

Sam opens the door just as I knock. "Hey, Katie. C'mon in." She opens the door wider, and I step inside. Their room isn't much different than ours, aside from the lamps on each nightstand and the posters hanging above the bed.

"You okay?" Amy asks, closing her book and placing it on a nightstand. "How did you even get our address?"

"We all got in a fight, so I figured space would be good," I say. "Your neighbor Antoinette told me you live here."

"Oh, her." Sam grimaces.

"She's no good?"

Amy rolls her eyes. "Not unless you like being called an Avenda. I mean, it's not like we *wanted* to be born in a Border town, right?"

"What exactly is an Avenda?" I ask. "This guy Anthony called Noah that yesterday down in the Activity Center. They almost got into a fight about it, too."

"Ah, the other Latrodectus," Amy says.

"That son of a—" Sam begins, standing up.

My eyebrows shoot up, and Amy hisses, "Language, Sam!"

"I have half a mind to go over there right now and give those little spiders a piece of my mind," Sam grumbles, sitting down, nonetheless.

"But we're not going to because we're better than those Ignavus fools," Amy says sweetly, putting her hand on top of Sam's. She turns to me. "Avenda means 'stranger.' It's a derogatory term that the soldiers born here like to call those of us who come in. The Latrodectus family is pure-born, or Meliors. It means nothing in terms of ranking or actual hierarchy, but it's a social issue that the Head Trainer has been trying to deal with for a long time."

"And Melior isn't a derogatory term?" I ask.

"Nope."

"Damn. Is there anything we can call them as a similar insult?"

Sam laughs a little. "We usually say Ignavus." Upon my look of confusion, she adds, "Coward."

"So, you guys are technically Avendas, too?"

"Yeah, but don't say that. We weren't born here, neither were you, but that doesn't mean anything."

I pause for a moment, thinking. "What's it like here, really?"

Amy answers me. "It's really hard. We have Sunday off to relax and chill, but most people spend it doing more leisurely training anyway. The camaraderie is like nothing else, despite the whole Avenda thing. Anyone here would die for anyone else in a heartbeat."

"Do you ever miss home?"

"Do you?"

"Yeah, all the time. I'm still trying to figure out if living here is better than living there. We all are."

"Where we come from," Amy begins. "Life was absolute hell. We were a working town, full of coal mines and factories. People were dying every day from respiratory failure, exhaustion, or beatings. When the Underground assassinated our officials, we had the option to come here or stay behind and try to rebuild our lives. Sam and I were the only two to go, and no matter how much it hurt to leave my family behind, I know it was the right choice. The Underground isn't perfect, but it's better than what we had before. It's better than all the other options."

"What happened to your families?" I ask.

"They died," Sam replies. "There's no way they survived. See, the guards from other towns always come and bomb the hell out of towns the Underground has taken over to try and kill us. Their own people don't matter to them, never have, and never will. It's just how it is."

"It shouldn't be."

"Well, that's why we fight. It's tough, but you'll get used to it."

"Yeah, but what's the *goal?* Will we have to fight forever, living underground like criminals?"

Amy and Sam glance at each other. Amy finds her voice first. "Well, the goal is to eventually rid the world of Borders so that all people can live on the Surface. We're labeled as terrorists by the government, but this is what we believe in, and the goal is that someday everyone will see the good in us and help us fight to win our freedom. Maybe the free people will even try to understand."

"There are free people?"

"Yes," Sam says, sighing heavily. "They live on the east coast of the country, aboveground. No Borders, no Matching."

"But... why?" I ask, head spinning.

"I—" Amy looks at Sam before continuing. "We don't know. Sure, there are theories, but we don't know why there are Borders here or why the country's western half has been annihilated. Where there aren't functioning Border towns, there are ruins."

I nod, trying to wrap my head around everything. I had no idea about... any of it, really. For half a moment, I wonder if they're teasing me, making this all up because I am a sheltered, confused, lost Avenda, but they're far too serious for that.

"It's a lot to take in, huh?" Sam asks, reading my mind.

"Yeah, it is," I sigh. "As if my life weren't confusing enough already."

"What do you mean?" Amy asks.

I take the opportunity to get away from Avendas and Meliors, from fighting and the Underground and the most terrible two weeks a person could have. I take the chance to be 17, just for a moment.

"What does it mean when... I don't know how to describe it, really. I guess he's just different. Chris, I mean. I feel stuff about him that I don't feel towards Noah. Is that normal?"

Sam and Amy smirk at each other as if to say *I told you so.* Sam answers my question. "I think you like him as more than just a friend. You've got that kind of freedom now; I say go for it and ask him out."

"I should?" I've never thought of actually being able to hold his hand, or kiss his cheek, especially in front of other human beings. Just the thought turns my stomach over.

Sam nods. "Yeah, if that's what makes you happy. Be happy, Katie; it's why you're alive."

———

AFTER SAM and Amy tell me about my new life and show me some sparring tricks ahead of time, I head back to the boys' room.

Chris is asleep on top of the covers, and it isn't even eight o'clock.

I smile, placing my key on the dresser and kicking my shoes off. I cover him with a spare blanket and get ready for bed in the bathroom, so the light doesn't wake him, thankful that he grabbed me a pair of pajamas and my own toothbrush. When I step out again, he's awake anyway.

"Katie?" He mumbles, voice sleepy.

"Yeah, it's me," I reply, sitting on the bed beside him. He lifts his head to look at me, running a hand through his scruffy hair as he blinks against the lamp's light.

"Are you okay?" he asks, and I nod. "Oh, okay. Good."

"Are *you* okay?"

"Better now," he pauses for a yawn. "That you're here."

I blush, but I don't think he notices. "Thanks, Chris. I'm better now, too."

CHAPTER ELEVEN

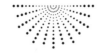

"Pistol training!" Cecilia yells. The second morning has us no more awake than the first. "I know two of you already know how to fire a gun, so I will trust you to teach these four how to *hold* one. No shooting until I say so."

Ava and I glance at each other, then walk over to Amy. Chris and Noah pair up with Sam.

"Okay, you guys get the basics, right?" Amy says. "Line up, take the safety off, pull the trigger."

I nod, and Ava says, "Yeah."

"So, we're going to practice lining up," she says, handing both Ava and me pistols. It's heavier than I thought it would be, and the metal is cold to the touch. "Safety on, of course. It's a paintball gun, but they still really hurt if you accidentally shoot yourself."

"What color do we have?" I joke, and she smiles. She told me last night that she uses these things called whitening strips that make her teeth whiter, and for whatever reason, having whiter teeth makes her smile prettier. They're perfectly straight, too.

"Blue today, I think," she says, tapping a small bump at the front of the gun. "You guys see this part here? That's the front sight. Here's the one at the back, too. Line up with those, like this." She spreads her feet shoulder-width apart, raising her gun at a target. I can feel Cecilia watching us.

"This is the part where you would take the safety off," she continues. "You do that by pressing this little switch up. Press it back down; safety's back on."

"Got it," I say eagerly. "Do you want us to try lining up?"

"Yeah, you guys can practice your stance, but keep your safeties on."

I spread my feet shoulder-width apart, my right foot slightly in front of my left, and take a deep breath. I rest my finger above the trigger, just like Amy did, taking another deep breath and raising my arms to shoulder height.

"I don't like this," Ava says, gun raised.

"Why not?" I smile, reveling in the slight burn in my shoulders and newfound power in my hands. "I think it feels good."

"I don't like how permanent it is if you fire it," she says quietly. "Once you do, you can't undo it." She is frowning, and naturally, I frown with her.

"But if you don't put your finger on the trigger, it has no power," I say, lowering my gun.

She returns to her normal posture with a sigh, gazing at her weapon in disdain. "This weapon means I can kill someone. I don't want that kind of responsibility."

"We use them way less than you'd think," Amy interjects. "It's very rare, trust me."

Regardless of whether she's telling the truth, Ava relaxes. "Oh, okay."

"You may fire!" Cecilia yells, and the frown returns to Ava's face.

"We'll be fine," I say before she can back down. "Like Amy said, we won't really have to use them."

She swallows hard, shifting from foot to foot and staring at the targets. "Okay."

"Alright, the gun will kick back a bit when you pull the trigger," Amy says. "You can't anticipate it, trust me. I used to do that all the time, and I would flinch just before I fired. My aim was thrown off, and I never once hit the target. Spread your feet apart to brace your-self for the kick, but don't pull away from it. I find it best to exhale deeply just before firing. Count to five as you breathe out and have your finger slowly pressing on the trigger. When you get to five, finish it out. Got it?"

"Yeah," I say.

Ava nods. "Got it."

"Go ahead."

My heart pounds as I turn toward the target, taking a deep breath to steady my nerves. I raise my gun, feet spread shoulder-width apart just like they told me, and click the safety off. I'm the first one to do so out of the four of us.

In. My parents would hate for me to do this. *Out.* Lucas would think it's cool. *In.* The bang would scare my mother. *Five, four.* This is my life, not theirs. *Three, two.* They can't control me anymore. *Out. One.*

I pull the trigger.

The gun lifts above me slightly as I fight to control the kick. My ears ring, and I open my eyes only to discover that I closed them.

"Wow," I breathe, looking at Ava and Amy. *"Wow."*

"Feels good, doesn't it?" Amy grins.

I glance at the target, unable to make out individual bullet holes. "Did I hit it?"

"Not even close."

"OKAY, I'M OUT," Ava declares that night. "No way am I going to kill people."

"We're required to be in combat for one year, that's it," Chris explains. He rubs a towel over his damp hair, still dripping with water from his recent shower. "Then we can apply for a transfer."

"How do you know?" Ava asks with a bite in her voice.

"Because the Head Trainer said so, remember?" Chris snaps back. "At our meeting."

"Oh yeah, the one where we had to specify what type of funeral we want. I definitely memorized the training rules since that was the most important part of that conversation."

Noah chooses that moment to enter the conversation, far more meekly than usual. "I've been reading up in the diary—"

"You went through my stuff?" I ask, turning to look at him.

"Ava let me in. You were in the shower last night, so I grabbed the diary. This is *nothing* like how Sophia described the world. She lived on the Surface, and Carcera didn't have a Border, and—"

"I've read it. I know what it says."

"Okay, chill; I know you're tired. Just hear me out, okay? Hayden, the guy across the hall, said the point of this place is to restore the world to what it was. If we can help them do that, then we should."

"Killing people shouldn't be the only way to do that," Ava grumbles.

"We already all have blood on our hands," Noah retorts.

"That doesn't mean I want more."

"Ava, it's too late for that!" Chris yells. "Our families are dead, all of them. Owen is dead; Melissa is dead. Our Matches will grow old and die alone, which is our collective fault because we *all* ran. If we hadn't done that, Noah and I would still be at home, and our families would still be alive. Think about that next time you hold a gun; maybe you'll be able to fire it."

His anger is met by stunned silence from the three of us. I've never heard him shout before.

"Chris…" Noah says tentatively, reaching out a hand.

The dark-haired boy trembles where he stands as if a strong wind might blow him over at any moment. Tears well in his eyes, a sight which I have not seen since we were eleven years old.

The slight touch of Noah's hand is enough to break him. They grab onto one another, holding on for dear life, Chris's chest heaving as the total weight of what's happened to us crushes him.

I glance at Ava, who seems close to tears herself and wrap an arm around her. She sighs heavily, leaning her head on my shoulder for a moment. After a few seconds, she pulls away, exiting the room quietly. I know better than to follow her.

Noah, upon noticing that Ava is gone, glances at me. I nod, putting a hand on Chris's shoulder as Noah slowly detaches himself to go after Ava. We've always been wordless, like that.

I stand on my toes and wrap my arms around Chris, letting him cry into my neck.

After several minutes of hiccupping sobs, he finally speaks. His voice is tight, and his breath catches in his throat. "They were everything I had."

"I know. I know."

"It's all my fault."

"Hey, Chris, no." I pull away to look at his face, holding him by the shoulders. "It's not your fault, and it's not mine. It was awful; it *is* awful. But we have each other. The four of us came out alive. What else can we do but fight?"

He shrinks away, trying to hide his face, but I cup his cheeks with my hands and force him to look at me. I remember what I told him after his father died.

"The time will pass. It must. The only way out is through."

He nods slightly, closing his eyes as another wave of grief overcomes him. "Okay."

We sit on the bed—his bed—and I wrap my arms around him, finally letting myself mourn as well. I cry for Lucas and all his plans, the things he wanted to accomplish, the people he wanted to love. I cry for my mother and all the students that will never see her again. I cry for my father and his dirty hands and the quiet, empty house he made home. I cry for our Matches, even Preston, all doomed to live alone now that we are gone. I cry because, despite everything, I still want to go home.

I think of the funeral we attended only a week or so ago. We had thought it selfish to cry at one's own loss because we weren't truly the ones suffering. We had thought the dead had suffered, had *their* lives cut short. Oh, were we wrong.

Time passes because it must, although it's hard to say how long we sit together. Eventually, we run out of tears, and then we are hollow shells clinging to each other. Chris pulls away to study my face, then turns and pushes me down, so we lie next to one another. He buries his face into my neck, draping one arm over my stomach and letting out a shuddering breath. After the initial shock of such intimacy leaves me, I turn slightly to hold him.

"Do you think we'll ever leave?" Chris says quietly. His voice is laced with exhaustion and fear—the voice of a young boy who just lost his father.

"What do you mean?" I realize that my fingers are involuntarily and instinctively tracing circles across his back, drawing them with my nails.

"Do you think we'll ever live aboveground again? Like before, only not inside a Border?"

"Well, I hope we're never on the run again because that really sucked. But I don't know if we'll ever live on the Surface again. I guess that's what we're fighting for."

His muscles eventually give in to sleep's warm embrace, and only then do I notice how tense he was.

"Hey, Katie, you okay?" Noah is kneeling next to the bed, and concern is etched into the lines on his forehead.

"I'm good."

"Fall asleep?"

"Mhm. What time is it?"

"7:45. You should get back to your room. Ava's missing you."

The detachment of myself from Chris is agonizingly difficult. He clings to my t-shirt in a nearly heartbreaking way, with an expression so innocent you could mistake him for being three years younger. Sleep-muddled mumbles escape his lips as I pull away, one hand reaching out. I tug one of the blankets loosely around his shoulders and resist the urge to crawl back under it with him.

"She okay?" I ask Noah.

MATCH

He shrugs. "I guess. She cried."

"So did he."

"Did you?" he asks, even though he already knows the answer.

"I saw Chris crying. What do you think?"

He gives me a sympathetic half-smile. "True."

I refrain from asking if he cried because I know he didn't. When we're upset, Noah can't cry with us. He has to fix it, so he blocks out his own emotions until we're okay again. He'll cry later, and that's the way he likes it. For as loud and involved as he can be, he's a shockingly private person.

"I'll see you in the morning?" I finally tear my eyes away from Chris to head to the door.

"Yeah. Katie, wait."

I pause at the door, one hand on the knob, poised to go.

"You're different to him than Ava is, you know that, right? He sees you differently."

My heart bottoms out of my chest. "How so?"

"Well, you don't see him fast asleep next to her."

"Oh." The word leaves my mouth like a squeak.

"Yeah."

"Goodnight."

"Night."

I exit the room and blink against the harsh light of the hallway. Ava is sitting on her bed when I get back to our room, eyes puffy and red.

She stands to greet me. "Katie, I'm so sorry about—"

I pull her into a hug before she can finish, too overwhelmed to talk anymore. "I'm sorry, too. We good?"

"Yeah, of course. You okay?"

I nod against her shoulder. "Yeah. You?"

She shrugs and pulls away.

"Hey, I know this has been really hard on all of us, but just know I'm here for you. We all are."

"Thanks." The small smile that graces her lips is enough to make me worry a little less. "You homesick yet?"

"Have been since the day we left." I step into the bathroom to brush my teeth. "How about you?"

"I wasn't for a while. Too busy worrying about staying alive. But now that we're here and safe…"

I know what she means. Now that we can let our guard down a bit, emotions flood our thoughts. Physical survival was only half the battle, and it's looking like that was the easiest part.

"The guys aren't making this any easier," I say after spitting my toothpaste into the sink. "Chris with his hair and his face and…"

"You like him." She says it as a fact, not a question.

"I guess that's what this is." I shrug and sit down on my bed cross-legged. "He fell asleep after crying it out."

"Somebody get cuddly?"

I laugh at this in spite of how much it broke my heart. "He's actually… I don't know. There's this weird highlight over him, like the rest of the world is black and white, and he's this bright green color."

"I feel the same way about Noah," she says. "He's just *different*. When he puts his hand on my shoulder, I feel like I'm on fire, but that doesn't happen with anyone else."

"I guess that's just the thing about… whatever this is. It's just different."

She finally smiles for real, even though she tries to suppress it. "We need sleep."

I raise one eyebrow but don't try to change the subject back. "Yeah, we do. Been a long day."

"I have a question." She swings her legs under the covers.

"I have an answer."

"If we were still at home, would you feel this way about him?"

I pause for a moment to think about my answer. I haven't really thought about that before. If we were still in Carcera right now, I wouldn't be allowed to feel this way. I probably wouldn't even be able to identify these feelings, but now that Sam and Amy have described it, I think I know what's going on. Now the question is: have I always felt this way? Has Chris always been this highlighted person in my life? I always preferred hanging out with just him over just Noah, but that seemed to be an occurrence based on availability and distance. I know Chris better than Noah, but just barely, and that's largely based on the amount of time we've spent together over the last few days alone. I've talked to him more than Ava or Noah, just like Ava is talking to Noah more than the rest of us. When did that change?

"I think I always have."

MORNING THREE BEGINS with classroom studies, so we get a break from early-morning runs. Chris doesn't say much, but I attribute his silence to how tired he must be.

"Sign language is a vital skill for all soldiers, regardless of their squad," Cecilia prompts. The first two days were an introduction to the Underground—now we're getting some real work done. Even so, Sam and Amy aren't with us this morning, and I miss their confident presence.

"You will learn to speak in full and fluent conversations with your hands. This skill can be used underwater, from a far distance, and in situations where you must remain silent. Many soldiers also lose at least partial hearing due to damage from explosions and gunshots, so this is an easier way to communicate with them. Can anyone tell me what this means?"

Cecilia signs a rapid set of words with her hands that are almost too fast to distinguish. I frantically flip through the packet she gave us, but her hands were too quick to make sense of.

Noah raises a tentative hand. "You have a son?"

"I do, in fact, very well done. Do you know sign already?"

"No, ma'am, but a guy in our hall taught me a few things when we had some free time."

"Learning outside of class is highly rewarded, Grim. What did he teach you?"

Noah raises his middle finger, prompting Cecilia to widen her eyes in amusement. "I don't know, ma'am; he said to show you this. What does it mean?"

"Grim, I highly suggest you stop learning from this guy. You just cursed me out," she chuckles.

Noah's face glows bright red as he lowers his hand beneath his desk. Cecilia demonstrates a few basic signs, including *hello, please, thank you,* and *help.* We spend the morning practicing the alphabet and those. By lunch, I have a headache from staring at the small words of the informative packet.

Sam and Amy join us at lunch, both eating broiled salmon over quinoa, whatever that is.

"How was sign?" Amy asks, taking a sip of iced tea.

"Interesting," Ava replies carefully. "Do you guys know how to do full sentences?"

Sam answers with her hands. I catch the word, *yes,* but that's all.

Amy translates for us. "Yeah, we can do full sentences."

"Cool."

Sam signs *yeah,* and then a barrage of words we don't know yet.

Again, Amy translates her hands. "Yeah, some of us actually prefer this over English. I have damage in my left ear from an explosion, so I only have partial hearing. It can be easier to understand sign rather than asking you guys to shout. Depends on the situation, though."

"I didn't know that," Chris says.

We eat the rest of our lunch in silence, then depart for the pool.

"Have you guys ever been swimming?" Sam asks as we change in the locker room. Cecilia handed Ava and me swimsuits to use for now, but we'll have to buy our own. I can't believe I'm actually going to wear this in front of the boys.

"No," Ava replies.

"Oh, Jesus," Amy murmurs. "This'll be fun." She and Sam exchange a knowing glance that does nothing to reassure us.

I stare at my body in the mirror with a mix of shock, pride, and absolute horror. I'm so *naked* in this... no one has ever seen me this bare.

Sam steps up behind me, pulling her hair into a ponytail. "Hey, the best thing you can do is to be confident. Swimming is only half the battle today."

"What do you mean?"

"You gotta act confident in your skin, or else you'll be too nervous to do *anything*. Fake it 'til you make it. You'll get used to it quickly, I promise."

I exhale slowly. "Okay."

We exit the locker room, and my eyes immediately find the tiled floor beneath my feet. Sam nudges my waist, which is covered by a skin-tight swimsuit that comes down to my upper thigh and is held on by two thick straps and sheer force of will alone. When I glance at her, she mouths, *Confidence,* then nods her head towards the guys.

My eyes follow her gaze, and my whole body flushes red. I'm practically naked, but they're practically naked too, even more so than us. I try to keep my focus on their faces, but it's tough when I can see parts of them that I've never seen before. I didn't know Chris has a birthmark just above his left hip.

"Okay, today we're going to start with floating." Cecilia sits in the lifeguard chair, wearing the same bathing suit we girls are wearing.

"Enter the pool by the stairs and take a few minutes to get used to the temperature and feel of the water."

We hesitantly enter the water, letting Sam and Amy go first. They walk right in, which gives me the boost of confidence I need to follow them.

The water feels smooth around my legs; even though I've had baths before, this is nothing like that.

"Guys, it's not too bad." I glance up at my friends. "C'mon in." Even though I'm only up to my knees on the stairs, I feel somewhat braver. I went in before the other three, after all. I wade in until the water tickles my waist, Noah right on my heels. He winces as his hips hit the chilly water. Chris and Ava follow next, moving slower than us but still coming in.

Soon the six of us are standing in the waist-high water, still trying to figure out how we feel about it.

"Alright, Sinderfield, you show them how it's done once I explain. We're going to float now. Lie on your back in the water and focus on keeping your breath even. You won't drown as long as you stay still and breathe," Cecilia says.

We glance hesitantly at her, but Sam and Amy quickly pop onto their backs as if lying in bed. After a moment, they stand up and walk over to us.

"I'll spot you," Sam offers to me. "Here's my hand. Put your lower back against it. Then kick your legs back and just breathe."

I follow her instructions carefully, staring up at the high ceiling and resisting the urge to kick my feet. And I'm floating in the water now, weightless and unafraid, ready to take on the world.

Little lights in the ceiling look like stars, making me wonder how much the constellations will change before I see them again. And it makes me wish the lights were actual stars, that I was floating in the endless ocean with the gentle waves rocking me.

"Pick a place you want to go more than anywhere else in the world," Sam had said in her room a few nights ago. "Anywhere at all."

My mind thought of home first, the only place I had ever known, but I knew that couldn't be my answer. There's a reason I ran away in the first place.

"The ocean," I finally said.

Sam smiled. "That's mine, too. That's the place we have to fight for."

CHAPTER TWELVE

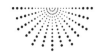

THE NEXT FEW weeks of training fly by, and I immerse myself in the physical brutality of it. My body is sore every morning, but it's a pain I quickly become accustomed to. We learn to lift, bench and squat and deadlift until we're so sore the next day that all we can do is foam roll and wince every time we move. We learn to swim properly like fish, gliding through the water. When that becomes normal, we even learn to fight at the bottom of the pool, to improve our strength and ability to focus without air. We learn basic first aid and CPR, and Chris excels at that. My favorite thing to learn is sparring, when we pop in mouthguards and wrestle one another, leaving purple and blue bruises all over. It's a welcome distraction from the homesickness that gnaws at us—while we haven't cried together since our arrival, I can tell in the mornings that Noah's eyes are often puffy, and Ava sniffles every now and again in the middle of the night.

One day, Cecilia changes up our usual pairings during a sparring session.

"Davis, you fight Grim," she calls. "Focus on your takedowns, not form."

Noah and I step into the ring and shake hands. I hope mine isn't trembling too much. Noah would never hurt me on purpose, but he could easily bust me up accidentally. With Ava or Amy or even Sam, it's always a pretty fair fight. This wouldn't even be a competition if we were to really go at it, and Noah sometimes forgets his strength. Chris's left eye is still green and yellow from a week ago.

"Ready?" I ask, bringing my hands up. The lack of boxing gloves makes me feel bare, but I also like being able to grab my opponent.

"Let's go," Noah replies, nodding once. I nod back, signaling the start of the fight. Noah doesn't move much, while I do. He likes to stay rooted to the spot, with his hands high to protect his face. I could stick a foot between his ribs right now, but I don't.

We study one another for a moment, trying to read the other's mind (which isn't all that difficult after over a decade of friendship). It looks like he wants to wait until I punch him, then use my arm as leverage to bring me to the floor.

I already know which move I'll use: the one that Sam taught me in the dorms one night. Noah's never been taught that, at least, I don't think he has. I'm no match for someone so much bigger than I am—not only is he ridiculously tall, but he's put on easily 15 pounds of muscle since being here.

My only chance is being able to outsmart him. Noah's not stupid, but he tends to lack finesse and can be clumsy sometimes.

He tries to grab me, but I duck and grab his arm with both hands, placing a foot behind his ankles. I sweep his legs out from under him and push him to the floor, where he lands with a far-too-satisfying thump.

The room goes silent; the rest of our squad stops what they're doing to stare at us.

Noah groans, propping himself up on his elbows. "Damn, Katie, where'd you learn to do that?"

"I pay attention." I extend a hand down to him. He takes it, pulling himself to his feet and literally shaking the impact off.

"You good?" I ask.

He grins. "My turn."

"I CAN'T WAIT for the Spring Festival!" Amy says, setting her tray down next to mine at lunch that same day.

"What's the Spring Festival?" Ava asks, twirling a metal fork through her spaghetti. I notice then that we all have different silverware —they must've been scavenged from different places on the Surface.

"It's a party to boost morale," Sam explains. She twists the cap off her Gatorade, a drink that helps replace the electrolytes in your body. I haven't tried one yet, although she recommends drinking it after a session in the weight room or a long run.

She continues. "All the adults get a party when the seasons change on the Surface. Kinda reminds everyone what we're doing this for, you know?"

We all nod.

"It's so much fun," Amy interjects, the words rushing from her mouth in excitement. "You'll even be allowed to drink alcohol. I'm not a big fan, but some people enjoy it." She shoots a playful glare at Sam.

"What's alcohol?" Noah asks, shoving another bite of dressing-drenched salad into his mouth.

"You don't know what alcohol is?" Amy says, and Noah shakes his head. "For real?"

"Nope," Chris says, taking a sip of water.

"Man, I thought *our* Border town was strict," Amy mutters. "You guys really lived in the dark."

"It's an adults-only drink," Sam explains. "It burns a little when it goes down your throat and can make you feel kind of dizzy and sick if you drink too much. The right amount is nice, though. You feel good."

"What else have you guys been deprived of?" Amy jokes. "Nail salons?"

"They have salons for our fingernails?" Ava asks, examining her bitten beds and torn-up cuticles.

Amy sinks her head into her hands. "What are we going to do with them, Sam?"

THE GIRLS, bless them, take us *shopping*. We learn about makeup, heels, dresses, and wearing the proper underwear if your dress is tight versus flowy. At one point, Sam holds up a lacy black pair and suggests I wear it for Chris, and mortified isn't a strong enough word to describe how I feel. I buy them, though, just to see how they'll look.

A few days later, the Spring Festival arrived. The four of us girls get dressed in my and Ava's room while the boys are getting ready in theirs.

"There," Sam says, taking the cool eyeliner brush off my face. "All done." I blink my eyes open and glance in the mirror.

"Wow," I breathe, staring at my reflection. "I look... wow."

"You like?" Sam asks, putting dark red lipstick on herself. It makes her look so much older.

"Love it." I grin, grabbing my dress from the door and stepping into the bathroom to change. It's black, tight, and short. The skirt flares out a bit to give me some breathing room, and the open back shows off my new muscles.

When I step out again, everyone is ready. We meet the guys in the hallway a few moments later, ankles slightly wobbly because of our heels.

"Wow," Chris says. "You look really nice."

"You look pretty good yourself." I smile, squeezing his arm as we begin the descent into the stairwell. Going down the stairs in heels is much harder than I anticipated, even though I practiced walking in the room.

Inside the dining hall, paper lanterns hang from the ceiling to create a warm glow. Some tables are at the back of the room, leaving an immense open space. A food and beverage bar takes up most of the back wall, where a large group is gathered, eating and drinking. The same rough sound pours from the ceiling as from the makeup store.

"This is dancing music?" I ask as we follow Amy and Sam through the winding maze of tables.

"Yeah!" Amy shouts as a deep boom echoes from the speakers. "You like?"

"Yeah!" I shout back, a smile on my face. The booming noise

repeats itself in a steady rhythm, and I like the feeling of it in my stomach.

"Here is good," Sam says, stopping at a table in the back corner and setting her small bag down. She doesn't let go of Amy's hand the whole time.

"Wait," Noah says, noticing their obvious affection for one another. "Are you two... dating?"

Amy blushes pink. "You guys didn't know?"

"No," Ava says, and we all shake our heads.

"God, are you people blind?" Sam jokes. "You guys really don't know that we've been dating the whole time we've known you?"

"I thought girlfriend, for you guys, meant a friend who is a girl," Noah says.

I echo his sentiments. "We didn't know girls were allowed to date girls."

"Hell yeah!" Sam shouts, raising the hand intertwined with Amy's.

"Girls can date girls, guys can date guys, girls can date guys, or you don't have to date anyone," Amy explains. "Clear?"

"Yeah, totally," I say, and the girls lead us to the buffet for some dinner.

After we eat our fill, Sam decides it's time for us to try alcohol.

"Shots!" she cries, practically dragging us to the bar.

"Six shots of whatever's easiest going down, please," Amy says to the bartender, handing him her card. He swipes it in the machine and pours six small glasses of clear liquid. "Thanks."

"It looks like water," Ava murmurs, examining her drink in the dim light. She takes a whiff. "Whew, doesn't smell like it, though."

"Listen, it's good, I promise," Sam says, holding up her glass for a toast. "To the newest members of Squad 5609, who, all things considered, are doing a phenomenal job."

"Cheers to that," Amy says, downing her shot and coughing slightly, holding up her thumb to let us know she's okay.

"Drink!" she says when she regains her breath, waving us on. I tip my head back and pour the foul-tasting liquid down my throat, shuddering as it burns all the way to my stomach.

"Gross!" I say, placing my glass down on the bar and shivering again.

"Foul," Chris agrees, making a face and setting his glass down gently.

"Seriously?" Sam laughs. "I'll have another!"

Sam drinks her heart out while Amy teaches Ava and me how to dance to the music. There seems to be a lot of hip-swinging involved, accompanied by rhythmic clapping and arm movements. Ava learns much faster than I do, thanks to her background in ballet. She dips and sways to the music, making it up as she continues. I stand to the side with Chris and Noah and sip some beer, which is far more pleasant than what we drank earlier.

"Having fun?" Noah asks a breathless Ava as a song ends.

"A blast!" she yells, and we all cringe. "Shouting?"

I nod. "Mhm."

"Sorry."

The DJ turns his microphone on to address the crowd, lowering the pounding bass. "Alright, ladies and gents, time to slow things down." A slower, melodic song flows from the speakers, and dozens of people partner up. Amy and Sam sway to the music, bodies pressed together and foreheads gently touching.

Chris extends one hand. "Wanna dance?" A hint of nervousness is evident in his voice.

"I would love to," I reply, a smile breaking out on my face. I take his hand, perhaps more firmly than I should, but I can't bring myself to care as he leads me out onto the dance floor. We find a place as if we actually have a clue what we're doing. Well, maybe he does, but I don't.

"I don't know how to dance," I confess.

"You don't need to," he whispers as he pulls me close. "Just put your arms around my neck and follow my lead."

My waist burns with pleasant fire where he touches me, fingertips light and delicate. I can feel his skin through my dress. I loop my arms around his neck; he's taller than I remember. I never knew his skin could be so soft or that the little hairs sticking out of the back of his neck are soft, too. I am painfully aware of how tight my dress is and of the feeling of lace between my legs. Slightly embarrassed by the thoughts running through my head, I turn my gaze to the floor.

"Nervous, Katie?" he whispers, chuckling quietly.

"No," I say quickly, looking back up at him with the fire reaching into my cheeks. "Of course not."

"Whatever you say." He smirks. Man, his *face*.

I pinch the back of his neck while matching his expression. Maybe matching isn't so bad, as long as I'm matching him. "Shut up."

We spin slowly and quietly, our feet lazily shuffling across the floor until the last chord fades away.

His fingertips glide off my waist when the song is over, leaving my skin cold.

"I... you're good at that," I say, unsure what I'm supposed to say. "You practiced?"

He grins. "Noah gave me a few pointers. Really, Ava did, since she taught him."

"Ah, smart," I say, stepping back as the music grows loud again and a dance circle forms in the center of the floor. "I'm gonna grab a drink. Want anything?"

"I'm good," he says, rubbing the back of his neck. "I'm gonna hit the restroom."

"Have fun," I reply, instantly regretting that comment as I turn and walk towards the bar.

At the bar, I park myself next to Sam.

"Hey!" she says, wrapping an arm around me.

"Hi!" I reply eagerly. "I need a drink."

"Man, *do* you!" She turns to the bartender. "Can I get something fruity for my girl Katie here?"

"I don't need fruity," I say quickly. "Uh, can I have something that tastes kind of like beer but stronger?"

"Whiskey?" he asks, already pouring a shot.

"Thanks." I slide him my card and turn to Sam. "Just straight down, right?"

"Yes, ma'am," she says, nodding earnestly.

I tip the whiskey down my throat, shuddering as it passes over my tongue and burns my chest. "Oh, Ankou," I gasp, coughing as I set the glass down on the table.

"Atta girl," Sam says, patting me on the back. "What've you had tonight?"

"This, the vodka, one beer."

"I'm cutting you off after two more, okay?"

"No, I'm fine," I say, raising my hand to the bartender. "Can I get another?"

He nods, eyes a little wide. "Pretty good for an Avenda."

"Do I get a free drink if I call you a Melior?"

He laughs, sliding the glass over to me. "This one's on the house regardless."

I grab my card off the bar before taking the glass. "Thanks, Ignavus."

Sam roars with laughter as I down the shot, suppressing the coughing fit this time. Even the bartender lets out a chuckle, surprised at my boldness.

"Let's dance!" I say to Sam, grabbing her arm.

"Okay!" She shouts back, following me.

CHAPTER THIRTEEN

Truth be told, I don't remember much coherently after that. I know we dance for a while, joined by Ava and Amy. The swirling lights, pounding music, and warm sensation in my stomach disorient me, and I lose track of time and place.

The first legitimate thing that I register is Chris. He's saying something to me, face swimming into my field of vision, but I can't tell what.

"What?" I shout.

"Are you okay?" he shouts.

I stop dancing (I was still dancing?) to take stock. "...yes," I say slowly.

"You're like, *bright* red," he says, gesturing to his face.

I touch my cheek to find it hot and damp. "Oh!"

"It's getting late," he says. Only then do I notice that people are vanishing through the doors; what was once a packed dance floor is now populated by just a few stragglers.

"Let me get you home," he continues, offering me an arm.

I nod, accepting it. "Okay."

"I'll meet you at home," Chris says to Noah, who seems to be having a similar conversation with Ava. He bids adieu to Sam and

Amy, and suddenly we're through the doors and in the cool yet painfully bright hallway.

"Oh, stairs," I groan, feet aching.

"Want me to carry you?" he asks jokingly.

"No, just... hang on." I sit down and fight with the buckle on my left shoe.

Chris kneels in front of me, nimble fingers quickly undoing the buckle and slipping my shoe off. His hands sit waiting for the other one before I can blink.

"Thank you," I say quietly as he extends a hand, my shoes held in the other.

The cement is cold underfoot as we begin the walk upstairs. He leaves a hand on my back to keep me steady. The walk is endless, but somehow, we make it to our hall.

"Let me get you settled," he says, opening the door to my room.

"Mkay," I reply, suddenly very sleepy. I yawn, pawing at my back and trying to unzip my dress as he turns on the lights. The floor seems to pitch steeply from side to side, and my head is throbbing.

"Here, here," Chris says, tossing my shoes down and spinning me around, undoing the clasp on the back of my dress. One of his fingertips slides down my back as he unzips it; I feel him hesitate when he realizes I'm not wearing a bra.

"I'm drunk," I say stupidly.

"Yes, a bit," he laughs, pulling away. "Go put on some PJs; I'll meet you out here."

I grab the pajamas I'd laid out for myself and fight my way into them in the bathroom. I glance at myself in the mirror—messy hair, red cheeks, stupid grin. It's hard to believe how genuine my happiness feels in this moment, so I step back into the main room before I can think too hard about it.

"Here, I'll hang up your dress," Chris offers. I notice that he's turned off the overhead light and has instead turned on the lamp next to my bed. My eyes don't hurt so bad with its' warm, soft glow.

"Thanks," I say, handing it to him as I crawl into bed.

"You okay?" he asks, sitting next to me once the dress is safely in the closet. "Oh, your makeup."

"It's fine," I say, yawning again.

"No, I got it, don't worry," he says, leaning into the bathroom and wetting a few tissues. He sits next to me again. "Close your eyes."

I oblige, since they're all too happy to be closed, and relish in the feeling of him gently wiping the mascara off my eyelashes with the cool cloth. He holds my face still with one hand, and my heart leaps.

"All done," he says softly.

I blink my eyes open in time to watch him toss the tissues into the trash can by the door.

"Nice," I say, smiling a little. I yawn once more.

"Thanks." He smiles, too. "Ava should be back any minute."

"She'll spend the night with Noah." I'm not sure how I know that, but I do.

"Probably," he says. "Are you okay here by yourself?"

I nod hesitantly.

"Do you have boy clothes in your dresser?" He must see the look on my face.

"Bottom left drawer."

He disappears from view for a moment, then comes back in pajamas, sitting on the edge of my bed again and setting my water bottle down on my nightstand. "There's water here if you need it."

"Thank you," I say quietly. "For everything."

"It's just water," he laughs. "But you're welcome."

"I'm still drunk."

"Yes, you are."

"I liked dancing with you. That was my favorite part."

"That was mine, too. Now go to sleep."

"Okay." I roll onto my side, letting my eyes slide shut. "Goodnight."

His weight slips off the bed, and I hear him switch the lamp off. "Goodnight." He presses his lips gently to my forehead, and then I'm gone.

WE HAVE the next day off from training because it's a Sunday, but Wakeup still sounds. It forces me awake, and I can't fall back to sleep. I was dreaming about something bad—my body is drenched in a cold sweat, and my hands are shaking. Lucas was there.

Chris is gone, Ava in his place. I guess she must've spent the night here, after all.

I stumble into the bathroom to wash my face, still half-asleep and with a soul-splitting headache. My fresh t-shirt gets caught on my face as I pull it on, and I stagger back into the room while struggling to get it off my face.

"Good morning!" Amy bubbles, bouncing over to me. I wince, still barely conscious, and yawn.

"Morning," I mumble, grabbing a pair of socks and slipping them onto my feet, trying to keep my balance as my stomach churns. "When did you get here?"

"Just a minute ago. I accidentally caught Ava in her undies. Sorry, girl." She shoots Ava an apologetic smile.

"That's why you knock," Ava mutters, pulling her hair into a high ponytail. I notice that she doesn't twist it into a bun like she usually does.

"I'll remember next time, sorry," Amy apologizes.

"Amy thinks we should go exploring this morning," Ava says, giving me a glare that I know to mean 'not today.' My heart aches to do something fun, but my body feels destroyed. It might be as close to death as I've ever come.

"Where's Sam?" I ask.

Amy shrugs. "Hangover isn't going too hot."

"Oh. Why don't we all get breakfast and then check on her?" I don't know why I say it, considering even the thought of toast makes me wish I were kneeling in front of the toilet, but breakfast is what we do. The descent to the dining hall is so ingrained into my body now that my feet feel strange just standing here.

Someone kicks the door open, making me jump. "I'm here."

"Wow." Ava whistles at the sight. Sam's hair is pulled back in a messy bun, and mascara smudges cling to the skin around her eyes.

"Oh, shut it," Sam grumbles, walking in and leaving the door open for the boys, who enter behind her. She flops down on my bed, curling around the wad of blankets I'd left unmade.

"What do you wanna do today, Sam?" Noah asks, bouncing once on the foot of my bed, nudging her. He seems fine, and so does Chris.

She lifts her middle finger.

"Activity Center, some games?" Amy suggests. A devilish light shines in her eyes. "A nice, greasy, fat-filled breakfast?"

Sam turns her hand to point at Amy, then lifts her head up. "I love you, but that's just wrong."

Amy laughs. "I know, I'm sorry. Let's go get you some toast, c'mon."

AFTER BREAKFAST (dry toast and ibuprofen for Sam and me), we head to the Activity Center.

"Karaoke?" Amy asks, leading us over to a small booth. We don't even need to ask her what it is for her to explain it to us. "It's where you sing into the mic with another person; the words are up on the screen."

I nod. "Got it."

"We'll demonstrate," Amy says, then turns to a girl holding two microphones. "Our usual, please."

"You two don't wanna change it up?" the girl asks.

"Nah, that's okay. When you come from a place where music doesn't exist, it's easy to get attached to a particular song," Amy jokes.

They step onto a low platform, glancing at each other and smiling. The song starts up, and they begin singing as if none of us are even here. Their confidence is astounding.

When the chorus comes on, I realize why they picked the song.

"Ohh," Chris murmurs. "Because they've kissed each other, and it's about kissing a girl…"

"Yeah." I nudge him in the side, ignoring how fast my heart is beating and how our arms are just brushing. I notice everything about him, always, even when I try not to.

After karaoke, we play some dart and water-gun games. I'm horrible at both, but Ava and Chris excel. Chris wins a small teddy bear, which he gives to me. I blush red as I hold it, thinking of last night, how he wiped my makeup off, and how unfair it is that he got to kiss me, but I didn't get to kiss him.

"Dancing?" Sam asks, leading us over to that dance game we tried on our first night here. Anthony Latrodectus is operating it again, and Noah glares at him.

"Sure!" Ava hops onto the pad with Sam next to her, and Anthony starts the music without a word. I notice how he's leering at Ava again, with beady black eyes shining. Chris must notice it, too, because he puts a hand on Noah's shoulder, whispering something in his ear from behind. Noah nods without turning to look at him, face steely calm, and cruel.

Sam and Ava finish up, high fiving each other at the end. Noah seems to break free of his imaginary restraints and storms over to Anthony.

"Hey, eyes off her ass, or I swear on—" he begins, but Anthony cuts him off.

"Dude, she's got plenty to share," he says, staring pointedly at Ava's chest.

Ava moves to take a swing at him, but Noah punches him square in the left cheek before she can. Anthony staggers backward, bringing a hand to his face. Noah steps forward again, but Chris grabs him and pulls him backward. Noah fights against him, but it's no use—Chris is stronger, always has been. I grab Ava and follow the boys with Sam and Amy in my wake.

Sam halts after deciding we're a safe distance away. "Nice hook, Noah."

"That guy's a jackass," Ava grumbles. "Looking at me like that. And I could've taken him myself, by the way."

"Sorry," Noah says. "Didn't mean to steal your first fight."

"Whoever said it was my first?" Ava says, leaning against the wall of our small corner.

"You've been in a fight?" Chris and I say in unison.

"Yeah, a few weeks ago," Ava says, shrugging. "There was a girl in the knife room who almost impaled me while working on free throwing. It was last Sunday when I went down for some extra practice. She tried to punch me when I told her off, but I took care of it."

"Jesus, Ava, why didn't you tell me?" Noah says. I notice how he says 'me,' not 'us.'

"It was nothing. Two punches, and then I knocked her legs out. Katie, would you have told us if you got in such a minor fight?"

"Yeah, I would. Why didn't you tell us?"

She crosses her arms defensively. "I just didn't think it was that important."

Noah rolls his eyes, and Chris bumps him with his elbow to tell him to relax.

"Well, I'm not sure about you guys, but I'm gonna head over to the spa," Amy says slowly. "I know we all love each other, but maybe some time apart might be good."

"Lord knows we're up each other's asses every other day of the week," Sam says.

Amy nudges her. "On Sunday, really?"

"Sorry, sorry," Sam replies, taking her girlfriend's hand. "Spa?"

"Spa."

They leave our little corner first. Noah mumbles something about a haircut, and Chris hesitates before following him.

Ava and I are left staring at each other.

"You said you swept her legs?" I ask.

"Yeah."

"Awesome."

WE WANDER around the shops for a while, buying new shorts and some good sneakers. When we get back to the room, I take a long

EMMA GRACE

shower. Ava's on the phone when I step out again almost an hour later.

"Yeah, girl, I get it," she giggles. There's some incoherent mumbling from the other end of the line, and she laughs again. "I'll see you later, k? Alright, buh-bye."

As Ava hangs up the phone, there is a frantic pounding at the door. We glance at each other as I stand up to get it. She nods as I slide the chain onto the lock just in case it's someone we don't want to see.

I crack the door slightly, keeping it in place with my foot.

"Katie!" Noah yells, hitting the door again. I flinch away, and the door rattles against the chain. "Let us in!"

I close it, which is difficult considering he's pressing against it with what feels like all his weight, and unhook the chain. The door flies open immediately, and the boys tumble inside in a flurry of arms and legs.

I step back, giving them room to collect themselves and glance at Ava. She shrugs, used to Noah's theatrics.

"Look!" Noah pants. He hauls Chris forward, and the boy in question winces. I raise my eyebrows, and Ava stands up.

"Noah, these sleeves don't go up that high," Chris complains.

"Then take off the hoodie," Noah replies quickly. "C'mon, we gotta show them."

Chris rolls his eyes and tugs his hoodie over his head. Instinctively, Ava and I avert our eyes.

"You can look," Chris says. "My left shoulder."

Slowly, Ava and I raise our eyes. I do my best to keep my gaze away from his abs and focus my attention on his shoulder.

"Nice," Ava comments, and it is. The tattoo is small, just a set of initials inked under his collarbone. *J. A.*

"Your father," I say quietly.

He nods.

We stand in silence for another moment as I try to keep my eyes on the tattoo.

"Did it hurt?" Ava asks.

"Only pressure, really," Chris replies. "It burned a little, but I have ink permanently in my body. I think it's worth it."

"It looks really good," I say honestly.

He smiles. "Thanks, Katie." And my whole body erupts in goose-bumps at the sound of him saying my name.

CHAPTER FOURTEEN

I can't fall asleep later that night. Ava is out like a light, but I toss and turn until well after midnight. My mind races with thoughts I can't quiet, images of training and my family, mostly Lucas looking at me from behind the railing on the stairs. *Run. Go.*

When I can't take the endless ticking of the clock anymore, I knock three times on the wall. If I'm lucky, one of the boys is still awake. If I'm extra lucky, it's Chris.

Someone knocks back on the wall four times, so I pull on a pair of socks and quietly pad through the door.

The hallway is so much darker without the constant chaos of 30 young adults. I press myself against the wall and slip into the boy's room, shutting the door softly behind me.

"Couldn't sleep?" Chris whispers from the semi-darkness. It takes a moment for my eyes to adjust, but I see the crack of light from the bathroom door move just a bit. I press the door open and shut it behind me, sitting on the floor across from him.

"Neither could you; I imagine," I say. His hair is disheveled, and he's wearing an extra-large hoodie. The sleeves cover his hands, and my heart skips a beat.

"What's on your mind?"

I sigh and stretch. "Everything. What about you?"

"Today's March 22nd," he says quietly.

"You still miss him," I say, nudging his arm with my foot.

"Like it was yesterday."

We sit silently for a long while as one tear slips down his cheek. I want to comfort him, but I don't know what to do. All I want is to take his hurt away.

"He told me that he would bring me to work one day," Chris says, clearing his throat and breaking the silence that seemed infinite. "That I could take the day from school, and he would show me everything. He said maybe I could work there someday. I hadn't told him about wanting to be a doctor yet, so I said yes. He was so excited…"

"He loved you," I say.

"He wouldn't want me here," Chris says bitterly. He spits the words out. "He'd want me to stay with my Match and marry her, be a doctor, have two kids, and live a normal life. I don't… I don't even know if he'd like the person I am now, let alone love me."

"You don't know that."

"I left them behind. I left them all behind. My sister, my mother… they were counting on me, and I failed them. What kind of person am I?"

I pause for a moment before responding. "You're his son. And you tried your best, Chris. It's not your fault what happened to them, to anyone. He would love you, believe me. That's what parents do." My own throat grows tight at the thought of my parents, who loved me quietly, stoically, but loved me, nonetheless.

He doesn't say anything, just closes his eyes and tilts his face to the sky that is separated from us by a hundred feet of rock. I slide over to sit next to him, wrapping an arm around his shoulders and letting him lean on me, needing to be next to him as much as he needs to be next to me.

"They would all be proud of you for this," I murmur. "You're fighting for them."

"Thank you," he breathes shakily. He waits another moment. "Do you ever think about going home?"

"Every day," I reply. "You?"

"Less now that I used to," he says. "Do you think they still miss us?"

"Every day."

"ALRIGHT GUYS, GATHER ROUND," Cecilia says the following evening. We grab towels to mop up our sweat—she had us doing lightweight circuits to end our day. My shoulders burn so much that I don't know if I can lift my arms above my head, but it's a feeling I embrace.

"You guys are getting experienced enough to start going on missions to the Surface now. You'll go on a quick evening mission this Friday, four days from now. It shouldn't take more than three or four hours, but you still have to take it seriously. One of the solar generators broke, so you will be in charge of safeguarding the engineers that repair it. You'll leave at 6:00 and should be back no later than 10:00, assuming everything goes smoothly. I'll give you the full briefing sheet tomorrow, just wanted to let you know ahead of time. Any questions?"

"So, we're just guarding them?" Chris asks. "We don't have to kill anyone?"

"Not unless you're fired upon."

Ava looks skeptical. "And what are the chances of that happening?"

"Very slim," Cecilia says reassuringly. "Guys, this is literally just a test to see how you do while protecting people from a threat that won't even be there. It's just like a classroom quiz."

We all glance at each other to see if anyone speaks up, but no one does.

"Alright, if there're no more questions, you're dismissed for the night. See you all in the morning. We'll warm up in the track room."

Once we get back to our rooms and clean up, the real discussion begins.

"Who's excited?" Noah asks, flopping down on Ava's bed and bouncing a tennis ball off the ceiling.

I vigorously rub a towel over my damp hair. "For the Surface mission? Hell yeah."

"You're not a little nervous?" Ava says to no one in particular.

"No, you?" Noah asks.

"Eh, little bit."

He sits up and wraps an arm around her—she gratefully leans into him. I glance at Chris, but he's busy not noticing.

"Look, you got nothing to be worried about. The three of us will be there the whole time, not to mention Sam and Amy. They're two ultimate badasses; we're totally safe," Noah says reassuringly.

That gets a smile out of her. "True, true. I'm pretty excited, actually."

"It's been weird not seeing the sun," Chris says. "And grass."

"Trees," I add. "Miss those."

"And weather," Ava says. "How weird is it to never feel wind?"

"Too weird."

"I can't wait to go back."

"Me neither."

WE'RE ready to go a few days later, waiting in the side room off the dining hall just like our briefing sheet said, at 6:00 PM on the dot. We're the only six people in the tiny room, and it's still cramped.

"Anybody nervous?" Sam asks.

"Not really," Noah says. "More excited than anything else."

"Same," Chris says. Ava and I nod in agreement.

We sit on the table with nothing more to say until the Head Trainer comes in a few minutes later.

"Good evening, 5609." His deep voice fills the room. "Are you ready to go?"

We stand at attention, Sam replying for everyone. "Yes, sir, we are."

He nods. "Good. I trust your trainer has briefed you?"

Sam answers again. "Yes, sir."

"Alright. If you would please follow me." He turns and exits the room through another side door I hadn't noticed. We follow him down a dark hallway that somehow makes me feel even more underground. The walls are jagged and rocky, and the air feels perpetually moist.

"Are you nervous?" he asks as we walk.

"No, sir," Chris says. "Looking forward to being back on the Surface, really."

He chuckles. "That's good. This isn't a hard mission. Just stay on your toes."

"Of course, sir."

We emerge into a brightly lit tunnel. I have to blink a few times to let my eyes adjust to the harsh light, but then I see the cars in front of me, and I forget about the blue spots dancing in my vision.

The cars are big hunks of metal with short doors and windows on either side. They're taller than I imagined, with glass windshields that come up to the frame for a roof that isn't there. They remind me of busses, only more compact, made for rugged terrain and traveling cross-country.

"You will be in Vehicle 36 with the two engineers. Their names are Paul and Ryan," the Head Trainer says. "Earl will be driving you, and I believe two of you have already met him. You have the morning off tomorrow. Training resumes after lunch. Stay sharp."

"Thank you, sir," Amy says. He leaves us in front of the car with 34 painted in yellow on the side.

We follow the line to car 36, where a tall man meets us. "Hi everyone, I'm Earl. I'll be driving for you tonight. Y'all are the guards for the engineers, right?"

"Yes, sir," Amy replies. "Good to see you."

"You too, Amy. And you don't need to call me 'sir,' we've been over this. Last time I saw you, you were passed out in the back of my car. You're good now, right?"

"Healthy as ever," she says, cracking a smile.

They make small talk for a few minutes as we wait for Paul and Ryan to arrive. The two of them are identical twins, which makes my chest ache. Lucas and I weren't identical, but we definitely looked alike. Sometimes I hated that feeling like we were tethered to each other rather than having our own faces, but now I miss resembling someone.

Paul and Ryan don't say much as we climb into the car, signing discreetly to each other instead of speaking.

"You guys ever been in a car before?" Earl asks, and we shake our heads.

"Just a bus, sir," Noah says.

Earl looks at us in the rearview mirror, goggles slightly askew and smushing his gray hair. He must use them to keep dirt out of his eyes since there's no roof. "Alrighty then, it's not much different than that. The engine's pretty loud at first, don't worry yourselves. It'll die down in a bit. Ready?"

"All set, Earl." Amy grins, and he smiles back. He's missing one of his front teeth.

The engine roars to life, and then the car begins to roll down the tunnel, which grows darker as we move. Eventually, we are consumed by total blackness with nothing but dim headlights to guide Earl to the exit. After several minutes of hushed rumbling, a pale light begins to grow in the distance. I look at Chris to discover that I can see him in the same way I did all those years ago in my attic; pale eyes staring at me in both wonder and fear, hair so dark it blends into the air around him.

I smile to reassure him, turning to face the front again. The light grows until suddenly we are bathed with fiery evening sunlight so bright it is nearly blinding.

I can't contain my laughter at the feeling of sunlight on my face, a warmth I haven't felt in so long. Chris lets go of my hand to reach his fingertips towards a sunset so big that my eyes can't see all of it at once. The grass spreads out in a sea of gold that ripples in the breeze, and mountains to the west cast long blue shadows over everything, slowly turning the day into night. There has never been anything this beautiful.

"We'll be there in about 20 minutes!" Earl shouts over the wind. "So, sit back and enjoy the view."

My best friends and I look at each other with nothing but pure joy. I didn't realize how much I had missed the sky.

The golden evening slowly fades to dusk, the brightest stars finding the strength to peek through the wispy clouds. Night closes in around us, but the dark doesn't scare me anymore.

"Almost there," Earl says after a little while. "5609, grab your weapons from the box behind my seat. Everything's loaded and ready to go for you."

Sam is the one to open the box, handing us each a rifle. My eyes widen when she hands me my gun; we've used the paintball versions, but never the real ones.

Earl brings the vehicle to a stop next to a copse of trees. "Alright, guys, I'll be back in two and a half hours to pick you up. If you need me before then, Paul has the radio. This is an easy task, nothing to worry about."

"Thanks," Amy says quietly, hopping out of the car and giving us all a hand. We echo her, and either Paul or Ryan leads us into the trees.

Crickets scream from all sides of us, the occasional bird adding to the cacophony. The world is much darker here, almost enough to frighten me. Almost.

"So, we just have to rewire some things in the generator," Paul or Ryan whispers. "It's not a hard job, and we're not that valuable, so I don't know why there are six of you, but if someone could hold the light, that would be great."

"Sure thing," Ava offers. "Are you guys from the Surface, originally?"

"No," he says. "We were born in the Underground. Our dad was an engineer, too, so he taught us everything about it. When we turned 16, they put us straight into a tech squad, said we were needed there more than anywhere else."

"Why 16?" she asks.

"That's the age you start training if you're born here. Usually, you spend at least four years in some combat squad, then most people transfer. Some take a break and then return to active duty, but you have to be done nine years by the time you're 30."

"What happens if you found the Underground and started training late?" Ava asks. We're coming up on the generator now, a giant black box taller than even Noah.

"Same rules unless you turn 30 soon. So, you guys will have to do nine years, but if you got here when you were 25, you'd only have to do 5," he replies. "Alright, hun, can you hold the light for us?"

I can see Ava blush even in the dark, and Noah puts his free hand on her waist.

"Ah, got it. My bad, I didn't know."

"Hey, no worries." Ava smiles and shakes Noah off. "So, what are you guys trying to fix?"

"A small receiver broke inside the box. It tells us how much energy has been collected. It's been going haywire for the past few days, and it usually fixes itself. Mostly it does that when there's a bad storm, but there hasn't been any nasty weather recently. The worst is in the summer, with those huge thunderstorms."

"Yeah, those are always intense," Ava says. The four of us simultaneously remember when we got stuck at school during a hailstorm. We were 12, and Chris was scared of the sound of hail on the roof. I know we all think about it because everyone looks at Chris, who takes a sudden and striking interest in his shoelaces.

Ava holds the flashlight for the two brothers, who communicate solely in sign language. The rest of us take up positions around them, staring out into the dark with nothing but the light of the almost-full moon to see by.

It's one of the most boring things I've ever done. Sam tells us not to talk because it's too distracting, and it's too dark to sign without a light. We can't do anything but stand in complete silence and stare into complete blackness.

My thoughts turn to my future. What will I do after training? Where will I go? Will I stay in combat until I age out, or will I want to do something else?

I know Chris will want to work in the hospital, and Ava loves to cook. I wonder if she would be interested in something with food, maybe coming up with new things for us to try. The food here is pretty good, if a little routine, for being chemically grown. I could see her adding her own flare to it, giving us a better rotation.

Sam and Amy will probably become trainers—they both have the qualities for it. Amy's good with kids—she might teach little ones in school. Noah will find a way to keep training his entire life, working in a tech squad, because he's Noah, and he always finds a way to do what he wants, and he loves stuff like that.

Me, though, I have no idea what I'll do. I like exploring in the library, so maybe I could do something there. I like being active, so perhaps I'll try to oversee a combat squad.

It's strange to think about a future I can choose, how I'll be able to decide where to go, what to do, and who to be. My options growing up weren't very extensive, and I already knew how many kids I'd have and the person I'd have them with. I may not even have kids now, or maybe I'll have three. I can marry Chris, or someone can waltz into my life tomorrow, and I can marry him instead. Hell, I can marry a her if I want to. Or I don't have to marry anyone—Cecilia never mentioned a spouse, although she wears a ring that Sam refers to as a 'wedding band,' and she has a child who joins us from time to time in classroom studies. He's smart, better at sign than I am, and adorable.

I have so many choices that sometimes it feels like too much, like the world is overwhelming, and I don't know what to do. Sometimes I wish someone else would choose for me, but then I remember that choice is a privilege, and I should be grateful for my freedoms. Sure, I can't really decide what training I'm in right now, where I live, or sometimes what I eat, but I get to determine a lot more than I used to back in Carcera. The Underground isn't the complete picture of freedom I had envisioned, but then again, I guess total freedom might not be a good thing. We need rules in life to keep us safe, despite what we may want.

A snap in the bushes catches my attention for a moment, but then a rabbit hops out, and I relax again. There's honestly nothing going on; are all missions to the Surface like this? Cecilia trained us like we were going to face death as soon as we got up here, but even reading about the genetic code of field mice wasn't as boring as this.

Noah kicks a rock across the ground, Amy sways gently to music that isn't playing, and Chris's eyes scan the trees relentlessly.

An hour passes, maybe two, but the sky gets progressively darker until it's almost impossible to see the trees in front of me. The talkative brother speaks up just when the darkness starts to become frightening.

"Alright, guys, it looks like we're all set. Everyone ready?"

We all agree it's time to go, and he radios for a ride; I finally realize he is Paul. Twenty silent minutes later, we can hear the roar of the car coming towards the trees, using the flashlights on our rifles to find our way out. Earl is all smiles when we arrive and climb aboard, returning our guns to the box.

"All set?" he asks. "How'd it go?"

"Should be good for a while," Paul says.

On the way home, we talk about what it was like growing up in the Underground and how they learn how to respect commands and be fully attentive from the very moment they start school. I shudder at the thought of five-year-olds in these olive-green uniforms.

The girls wear thick green tights that come down over our feet, and the boys wear pants of the same color that tighten at the ankles. Everyone has a pair of black combat boots and a black jacket over a beige t-shirt made of the same material as our pants, which can slow most bullets and is waterproof as well as fire-resistant. Sam told me that these things are virtually indestructible; of course, it may not be able to deflect a knife or a point-blank bullet, but it'll be hard to get anything through enough to kill you.

Paul tells us about growing up here. "The first thing we learned in school was how to treat each other with absolute respect, no matter our mood. That always came first, cause one day we were gonna be comrades, ya know? We went to class every weekday with the same 20 kids; sometimes, we would work with some other classes, but it wasn't that common. We learned all our math and the history of the Underground and how to read, but a lot of it was about mechanics, agriculture, and war as we grew up. The kids that grow up here... they see some shit. Ryan works in the hospital on Sunday nights, has since we were 12, and he's seen it all."

You volunteer at the hospital? Chris signs to Ryan.

Yeah, he signs back.

The two of them continue in a rapid-fire sign conversation while the rest of us sit in silence and look out at the night. I tilt my head back to gaze at the stars and let the pale moonlight wash over me, more than happy to be back on the Surface. I try to ignore the dreaded feeling of approaching the tunnel, but before I know it, we're back in the Underground, saying goodbye to the twins, and heading back to our rooms.

By the next morning, it's like the whole trip was nothing but a dream.

CHAPTER FIFTEEN

THE DAYS PASS QUICKLY after our first mission. Chris starts volunteering at the hospital with Ryan on Sunday nights, and he loves every second of it. I get a small tattoo of the Gemini constellation on the inside of my left forearm and spend most of my free time in the library, researching ways to make medical supplies. Chris told me the hospital is low on gauze and pain meds. Ava finds an extra-curricular training course centered around ballet, so she's there Sunday mornings and Wednesday nights. We grieve when we can, but mostly we're too busy for anything other than a dull, constant ache. About another month passes uneventfully before things change again.

We're lifting in the weight room one day when Cecilia leaves us mostly to our own devices. Her son is in with us, playing with clips and 1-pound weights, mimicking Noah's movements as he works in the squat rack. Cecilia is going over paperwork on one of the weight benches, frowning every so often, and highlighting things.

"What do you think's going on?" I ask Sam as she prepares to spot me while I bench.

"Not sure," Sam says, looking over at our trainer. "It's weird that Tucker's here, and we're not in the classroom."

"He's been around a lot recently, hasn't he?"

"Yeah. I mean, I don't mind; look at him."

We glance over to see Noah and Tucker squatting in unison; after his set, Noah re-racks the bar and gives him a high-five. Tucker's gap-toothed grin spreads from ear to ear.

"How could you not want him around?" I ask, glancing over to where Chris, Amy, and Ava are training core. Ava catches my eye and winks, and I blow her a kiss. Chris, thinking it's for him, blushes red and smiles to himself.

"Right?" Sam asks, having missed what just happened. "Alright, you ready?"

"Yeah," I say, laying back and grabbing the bar. "You got me?"

"Yeah, duh."

I bench a few times, then rack the bar and sit up. Now Noah is working on his deadlift, and Tucker has found a paper towel roll to use as a makeshift bar.

"He's really good with kids, huh?" Sam asks, watching Noah teach him how to lift it properly.

"Always has been," I say. "His brother's only five. They were real close."

"It's a shame," she says.

"What is?"

"That his brother isn't here."

"Oh." I pause, thinking of Owen and his cheeky smile. "Yeah, it is. Do you have family back home?"

"Where, up there?" She nods to the ceiling.

"Yeah."

"Oh, I did. Older sister and my parents. C'mon, 'nother set."

I don't ask again, instead finishing my sets and then spotting her as she does hers. We train core after, trading with Chris, Ava, and Amy. Cecilia dismisses us before dinner is even open, so we head back to our rooms. She keeps Sam and Amy behind for a talk, which seems weird, but I don't question her. Still, it eats at me as we climb the stairs.

"I'm dying," Ava groans. She clings to the railing, using it to hoist herself up each step.

"Me, too," I say. "Do you know why she kept Amy and Sam back?"

"Maybe she's talking to them about new members," Chris suggests.

"Why would she talk to them about that and not us?" Noah says

"I don't know. Meet in the boys' room in half an hour," I say.

"Sure," Ava says, the boys nodding their agreement.

We split up in our hallway, and Ava sprints into the bathroom before I can make it there. I smile and roll my eyes, taking the time to clean the room. Ava finishes in less than fifteen minutes, and I hop in the shower, enjoying every second.

Twenty minutes later, I step back into the main room, fresh and clean, holding my ball of sweaty clothes in one fist. Ava's already left, so I kick on a pair of slides and walk over to the boys' room. As soon as I see everyone gathered, I know something's up.

Amy and Sam wear neutral expressions that poorly mask fear, while Noah paces and even Ava fidgets. Chris sits still but is breathing deeply, trying to calm something within him.

"What's going on?" I ask. "Is everyone okay?"

"We're going to the Surface," Sam explains. She begins slowly, and then the words tumble out her mouth like water across river stones. "For a mission in the Army Center. We are to go in at night and capture as many guards and trainers as possible before calling for a helicopter to retrieve us. We leave in one week, two days.

"It's going to be a challenging mission. You guys know the risks already, but they are going to be heightened based on the time frame and target. These are highly trained guards, and we'll do this primarily in the dark. Over the next week, make sure to work extra hard on sign."

Okay, I sign, throat too tight to speak. I'd be lying if I said I wasn't nervous.

Be back later, Sam signs.

The two girls exit the room, leaving the four of us to comprehend what we just heard.

"Is everyone okay?" I ask.

"Yeah, all good," Noah says quickly. "I'm gonna go get some food; you want me to bring it back?"

"I'll go with you," Ava offers. "Any special requests?"

"Can you grab me a Gatorade?" I ask, sitting down on Noah's bed.

"Yeah, sure. Chris?"

"Oh, I'm not that hungry," he says. "PB&J's fine. Thanks."

"No problem," she says. "Be right back."

Noah closes the door gently behind them, and then it's just Chris and me.

"You alright?" I ask.

"Yeah," he says slowly, clearing his throat. He sets to work, pulling out clothes for tomorrow and straightening up his already neat dresser. We've been here almost three months, and we still barely have any things that are *ours*.

"Worried?"

"A little."

"Talk to me."

"I don't want to talk about it, Katie."

I stand up and unconsciously place a hand on his arm. He stops refolding his shorts and turns to me, looking at me the way only he can. He looks at me like I am the moon, like I am the light in his sea of darkness, which is so wrong because he is *my* moon, he is *my* light. He looks at me like I mean the world to him, which I do because I'm his best friend. Nothing more.

I used to think that if we were ever sent to the Surface like this, it would be the perfect time to tell him how I feel. I used to believe that knowing the possibility of death would seal the deal, that I would tell him because it might be my only chance. I used to think that I would be brave, that I *could* be brave.

But now, I can't find the words to express myself. I can't put us through the pain of knowing that we could've had a chance if we had just swallowed our fear and *told each other*. I can't do such a horrible thing to him just to clear my conscience. He's my best friend, and I can't make him suffer just so I can die happy, should the worst happen. This is a nightmare.

I push my feelings down into my stomach, where I can usually ignore them. I try to tuck them away because everyone has always taught me that an unmatched relationship is nothing but destruction. I hide them deep within the recesses of my mind because this is just one more thing the government is right about.

They tell us unmatched, unplanned feelings are the enemy. All I've ever known is that unmatched feelings destroy people and lives. The government is right, and I know that because it hurts. It aches in my head and throbs in my stomach and burns in my throat. The weight of unsaid words is too much to bear. I can't think straight when he's near me; it's like thousands of guns firing all at once. I can't breathe with him in the room or in my head. I can't breathe, period.

This hurts because it's real, because it matters, and because it's Chris. The boy with the iced-over eyes, the nervous smile, and the messy hair that always falls over his eyes just right. The safe one, the doctor-in-training, the rational thinker, the glue that holds the four of us together. It's all of him. It's always been all of him.

CHAPTER SIXTEEN

CHRIS and I decide to check out the library's fiction section that evening. We both frequent the library but have never been over in that part. Reading a pretend story is something I want to do before I die, and I should probably get it done now, just in case.

The walk to the library is silent in a peaceful way. Halfway down the stairs, I stop fighting the impulse and take his hand. He glances down at our intertwined fingers and smiles briefly, but we keep walking without a word. His hand is warm.

The fiction section is infinitely larger than I imagined it would be. Hundreds upon thousands of books line the ten-foot shelves that stand in endless lines. I find a woman browsing and decide to ask her what we should be looking for.

"Hi, ma'am, are there any good fiction novels you recommend for first-time readers? My... uh, friend and I have only ever read nonfiction books. Anything good, you know?"

"Here, try these." She hands me two off her pile. "They're two of my favorites."

"I can go grab my own if—"

"No, you're fine, hun; I know where to find them, no problem. You and your friend enjoy, now." She gives me a warm smile and returns to browsing.

I give Chris the thicker book since he's a faster reader than I am. We set out in search of a table and instead find a small couch that is remarkably comfortable and forces us to sit remarkably close together. Our thighs brush as we crack the spines of our books and begin to read.

The language is foreign, and getting into the novel is difficult, to say the least, but the characters are interesting. I find it hard to believe they're not real. How can people write from the perspective of other people?

Before I know it, Chris and I are bound in a tangle of arms and legs that somehow results in maximum comfort. At one point, I glance up from my book to see that his mouth is terrifyingly close to mine. I would have to move less than an inch to seal the gap.

All too soon, we have to go, just when the story starts to get good.

"Curfew in 30 minutes!" a librarian calls.

"Guess we're wrapping up?" I sigh.

"Guess so," Chris says. "I gotta run to the men's room; I'll meet you at the doors where we came in."

I take his book and stroll through the shelves, taking the time alone to enjoy the quiet. I am so lost in thought that I don't notice Cecilia until I nearly run into her.

"Hey, Davis," she says. "Didn't mean to scare you."

"Oh, Cecilia, hi."

"Did Sam and Amy tell you?"

"Yeah. We're gonna start prepping extra tomorrow."

"I'll make sure you guys are ready. We can work a bit more on sign and knife skills."

I set my books down on a nearby table and decide to use sign to show her that I know it just fine. Using my hands to speak came far more naturally for me than for my friends. *Thank you, Cecilia. I feel ready, thanks to you.*

Thank you, Davis. Have a good night.

You, too.

We part ways, and I leave the books without any idea where else to put them.

Chris is waiting for me by the front doors, and as soon as I see him, he smiles.

"Hey," I say, taking his hand as if it were the most natural thing in the world. "Ready to head up?"

"Yeah, all good. Thanks for coming with me."

"Thanks for bringing me."

WHEN I GET BACK to the room, Ava is already in bed. She stares up at the ceiling as I get changed.

"Hey, Ava," I say once we're both settled in. I roll onto my side to face her. "You'd tell me if you and Noah were actually dating, right?"

"Well, yeah," she replies sleepily, rolling as well. "Would you tell me if you and Chris got together?"

"I don't think it's gonna happen," I sigh, drawing the covers tighter around my shoulders. I have no idea how she can sleep without blankets in this icebox.

"There's more of a chance than you think."

Suddenly I'm wide awake. "What'd he tell you?"

"Nothing."

"Ava."

"Nothing, I swear! You're just lucky I have eyes—I see how he looks at you."

"How would you describe the way he looks at me?" I ask heart caught in my throat.

She grins, pausing a moment. "It's gonna sound ridiculous, but... it's like you give him air."

We swim and run the next day. We swim for two hours, one of the most exhausting things I've ever done, and then we run five miles. By the time lunch rolls around, I am near collapse. We all are.

"What is she *doing?*" Noah pants on our way to lunch.

"Making sure we're ready," Sam says. "She did this last time, too."

Chris wipes his face with a towel, brushing damp hair out of his eyes. It sticks to his forehead anyway. "Feels more like she's trying to kill us."

"We need to be ready," Sam says. "She wants to keep us alive, not just for her own reputation. Believe it or not, she really does care."

"Yeah," Amy adds. "She's going to work us hard for a few days. Life's going to suck. But in those last three days, before we go, she'll actually go really light. Give us a break. Let us rest up. We'll do a lot of team-building exercises, working together to solve problems, that sort of thing. Many of the final few days are focused on mental readiness to give our bodies a break. We have the last day off to rest and pack our things. Say goodbyes and such."

"You make it sound like we're never coming back," I joke, attempting to lighten the mood. They all stare at me like I've grown an extra head.

"Alright, okay, sorry," I say, backtracking. "We have that last day off to hang out and rest."

"That's more like it," Sam grumbles as we push open the doors to the dining hall.

Deciding I'm not hungry, I grab a bottle of electrolyte water and reserve a small round table for the six of us. I sip my water quietly while I wait for them to arrive.

"Hey, this seat taken?" a boy asks, gesturing to the seat next to me. He has short blond hair and dark green eyes, the color of summer leaves.

"Depends," I say, setting my water down and leaning forward. "Why do you ask?"

"I'll answer that question when you answer mine," he says.

"It's taken," I say coldly. His gaze is too harsh, his hands too white-knuckled around his lunch tray. "Now, answer *my* question."

"I'm going to the Surface in a few days," he says. "I need some action."

"Action?"

"You know…" He thrusts his hips forward just slightly.

"Ugh, gross. Go find action somewhere else."

"What if I don't *want* to find it somewhere else?"

"Well, that's too bad, isn't it?" I spit, standing up. "I'm leaving soon, too; you don't see me trying to screw anything that moves."

With that, I turn and walk away, putting as much power into each step as I can. I think all is well for a moment; he won't speak to me again. But then, obviously not used to having a girl walk away, he yells something that pushes me over the edge.

"Hey, sweetheart! Don't you think we should get to know each other before we go? For the mission and all?"

I know those words too well. Preston said those same words to me, but that was a long time ago, in a different life. Preston Harper, the boy who forced himself upon me, choking me, stealing the very air from my lungs. The boy who kept me turning over my shoulder for years, who made me so afraid for so long.

"*What* did you just call me?" I quietly ask, coming abruptly to a stop.

"Sweetheart. It's a term of endearment." The boy makes a sympathetic face, setting his tray down. "Not very bright, are you?"

"Brighter than you."

"At least I know how to give you a good time."

At this, I snap.

"What do I look like to you?" I ask, stepping up to him. He's taller than I thought, but I don't care. "Do I look like a fucking sex toy? Because I'm not, and if you think talking to girls like that is gonna get you laid, boy, do you have some *serious* rethinking to do."

As I turn to walk away, he grabs my arm to pull me back.

Before he can speak, I punch him in the nose. The crack is oddly satisfying, but not nearly as gratifying as the blood that trickles his lips down only seconds later.

"Bitch," he growls, reeling back to hit me. I duck under his arm and dig my right elbow between two ribs where I know it'll knock the air from his lungs. As he doubles over, clutching his side in pain, I slam my right knee into his groin. He falls to the ground, and I stare down at him.

"Word of advice," I say, just loudly enough for the surrounding tables to hear. I enjoy the familiar rush of adrenaline coursing through my veins. "Don't ever call a girl a bitch, especially one with combat training. And kissing you would hurt far worse than the bullet I've already taken for the sake of our freedom. So next time you want to talk straight from your ass, try speaking English."

I stalk away, head held high as he moans in pain. Everyone is watching and staring, but I don't care. No one gets to objectify me. No one gets to scare me as Preston did ever again.

"Did you just kick that guy's ass?" Sam asks as I reach my group of friends.

"You know him?" I ask, still shaking as we take our seats well across the dining hall from the boy. It's hard to tell whether I tremble from fear or adrenaline—probably both.

"That's Dylan Parker, the greatest manwhore in 8. He does that to everyone, so don't take it personally."

"But thanks for giving him a beating," Amy adds. "He needed that."

"You don't think that could've been bad?" Chris says, taking a bite of salad. "I mean, what if he hurt you?"

"We don't specialize in combat for nothing, Chris," Ava says. "Good idea with the knee, too. I'll remember that when we're up on the Surface."

"Thanks." I smile as the tension slowly drains from my body. I watch as Dylan gets up slowly, collects his tray, and walks to his friends, looking awfully uncomfortable. He has the gait of a man who walks in pain but is trying to hide it to save the last of his dignity.

"What did he say to you?" Noah asks.

"Exactly what Preston said to me, and then some," I sigh. "He invited me over after training for... you know. Then he called me a bitch."

"When did Preston say that to you?" Ava asks, and I realize where I screwed up. I glance over to Noah, who is suddenly very interested in the pattern on the table.

"My last day of school," I confess. "He came up to me in the hallway, said I was pretty. He wanted to get to know me. He shoved me against my locker, and I bit his lip. Then he knocked me on the floor and kissed me again. Noah beat the shit out of him when he got there."

"Is that why your knuckles were raw in the woods that night?" Ava asks Noah in horror. She turns to me, "And you had a bruise on the corner of your lip?"

Noah and I nod. Tears of embarrassment spring into my eyes; how could I have let him do that to me?

Chris puts a gentle hand on my arm. "Hey, it's okay. He's an ass, but you're tougher than him."

I nod, slowly closing my eyes and pressing the tears away. "It was a bad kiss, anyway."

"Too much tongue?" Amy asks, and we all laugh briefly.

"Too much Preston."

"Huh," Noah says when we step into the classroom the following day. He stops short in the doorway, and I bump into him.

"Jeez, Noah, what?" I ask, standing on my toes and peering around his shoulder. "Oh."

We hesitantly step inside to where there are rope and CPR dummies lying on the desks. Cecilia sits on her desk at the front, inspecting her fingernails.

"Well, don't just stand there; take your seats," she says, looking up at us.

We slide into our seats; even Sam and Amy seem weirded out.

"Considering the nature of your next mission, I figured it's time for you to learn to gag and cuff with rope and towels," Cecilia explains. "We'll use the dummies to discuss the proper way to gag someone while leaving the airway open; then, I'll show you the proper restraints. Omenstat, you'll be my dummy."

Amy nods, and I notice how Sam glances at her, expressing mixed fear and relief.

Cecilia has Amy lie on the desks as if she were asleep in bed. "Now," Cecilia begins, holding a towel in her hands. "It's important that you gag your target *first*. If you just start tying their hands, they can scream and alert the others. Here's how you gag them properly—airway obstruction should be avoided at all costs. The point is to bring these soldiers back alive."

And then, seemingly without warning, she shoves the towel into Amy's mouth. Amy's eyes widen in surprise, and her chest heaves momentarily as she inhales through her nose. Sam twitches beside me, shoving her hands into the pockets of her leggings.

"And the element of surprise is key," Cecilia continues. "Omenstat here had no idea I was about to do that, which gave her no time to cry out. Now, Omenstat, can you breathe?"

Amy nods.

"Good. I want you all to think about them holding the towel in their mouths. I recommend tying it behind the head to keep it secure. To do that, simply roll the person—" she rolls Amy quickly onto her stomach; Sam and I wince at the thud of her forehead hitting the desk "—onto their stomach and tie a quick knot. Nothing fancy since we want to be able to get it out, and no bows. Those are too easy for them to get out themselves. Next, we tie the hands."

She grabs a rope and holds it up for us to see. Sam continues to fidget, and I notice how her leg twitches.

"Easy. Quick double square knot, nothing complicated," Cecilia explains as she works. "See how I have the palms facing outwards? That's to avoid strain on the shoulders--it keeps them comfortable, which is the least we can do. And you want the knot to be right at the wrists, with the palms apart. Double the knot, so it's harder for them to undo, and then cut any excess rope. I won't do that here for the sake of not wasting things, but you know what I'm talking about."

We nod, and I find myself wishing this could just be over.

159

"Next is the feet. You can use the extra rope from the hands, but grab a new piece if it's too short. Loop the rope three times around the ankles and then do the same knot. Ensure the toes are pointed the same way, and the knees aren't splayed out. Again, this will help to keep them physically comfortable and less likely to fight. And that's it, really. Omenstat, any concerns?"

Amy makes a strained sound in her throat, which prompts Cecilia to untie the gag and roll her over quickly.

"All good, quite comfy," Amy says. "Should we leave them face-down, or—"

"No, that was my mistake," Cecilia says. "Make sure that you leave them face-up so they can breathe better. And then evacuation teams will be there to bring them to the roof, so they'll make any necessary adjustments. Your job is to make sure they're simply not going anywhere. Any questions?"

No one says anything.

"Very well then. You all can practice gagging and tying on the dummies first. Then you're welcome to practice on one another. Let's pair up and go two people to a dummy so you can observe and critique one another."

We do as she says, breaking off into our usual pairings as she unties Amy. Sam is there as soon as Amy stands, placing one hand on her back and guiding her over to a dummy in the corner of the room.

Chris and I choose a dummy in the front, and Ava and Noah opt for one in the back.

"This is..." Chris says, holding a coil of rope in his hands.

"Yeah," I reply. "Okay, you wanna go first?"

He stares at me, half a smile on his face. "Fine."

Chris shoves the towel in the dummy's mouth and then flips it over, tying a quick, simple knot.

"Your turn," he says, untying it just as quickly and sliding the dummy to my side of the desk.

We quickly turn it into a game, seeing who can tie the fastest knot or the more complicated one. Soon it's as if the others have vanished, and we're in our own little bubble.

"Davis and Ashborrow, how about we try wrists and ankles?" Cecilia suggests from the front of the room.

"Sorry, yes, ma'am," I say quickly, cheeks growing hot.

"Here, I can go first," Chris says. "We can do this on the floor." He lays down before I can protest.

I kneel beside him, holding a towel and a coil of rope. "Should I gag you, too?"

"Might as well get the full effect," he says, shrugging. "Do your worst."

I grab the towel and pause for a moment, taking a deep breath. He grins at me, and I smile back, then stuff the towel into his mouth. I hate the way his eyes widen, and his chest bucks involuntarily, the thunk of his hip as I roll him over, and the way my fingers are shaking as I try to tie a knot.

Once the gag is secured, I reach for the coil of rope, but then Chris pushes himself up and effectively tackles me, straddling my hips and deftly untying the gag I'd worked so hard on.

My eyes are practically bugging out of my head as I stare up at him, both of us panting as he tosses the towel to the side.

"You're going to have to work a bit harder than that, Katie," he says quietly, studying me.

I say nothing. What is there to say when your best friend is sitting on your hips, and you can feel a heartbeat that you aren't quite sure is yours?

After a moment of silence, Chris lets out a little chuckle and then slides off me. "Again? I won't tackle you this time."

I prop myself up on my elbows and force out a laugh, too. "Fine. You promise?"

"Cross my heart."

"DAVIS, HANG BACK," Cecilia says after training. My friends file out the door, and I want to groan at the thought of having to wait until after Ava to shower.

I expect Cecilia to ask for my help putting away the dummies and rope, but instead, she sits at one of the desks, gesturing for me to sit across from her. I oblige, wondering if this is how Noah felt every time he got in trouble at school.

"Tell me about Ashborrow," Cecilia says, not unkindly.

"What about him, ma'am?"

She holds up a hand, taking a deep breath. "And cut it with the 'ma'am,' please. That was just for the first few weeks to make you think I was in charge."

"Oh, sorry, m—" I stop myself. "Sorry."

"That's quite alright. Now, for safety reasons, I need to know the nature of your relationship with Ashborrow."

"We're just friends," I say, voice strained more than I'd like it to be.

She arches her eyebrows in the same expression my mother used to make, and I feel uncharacteristic tears spring into my eyes.

"Just friends," I repeat, clearing my throat. "I... I used to want to tell him, but..."

She waits patiently, but no more words are willing to force their way from my throat.

I shake my head, sniffling.

Cecilia stands, walks to the back supply closet, and gets a box of tissues. She sets them on my desk and then returns to her seat as I dab at my eyes, the way my mother used to when telling a story about a particularly unlucky or unloved child. Will all women always remind me of her?

"I'm just so scared," I blurt out, hiccupping as I try so hard not to sob.

"Of?"

"If I tell you how I feel, will you send him away?"

She laughs a bit, gently reaching across the aisle and squeezing my forearm. "Davis, no. I will never separate you from any of them, nor any of them from you. I just wanted to know for safety reasons."

"What does that mean?"

She sighs. "There might be some missions in the future where I send him without you."

"But you never split up Sam and Amy."

"There's no chance that either of them could be pregnant."

The look on my face must say it all, because she quickly continues.

"I was going on missions until I found out I was pregnant, which was quite late," she explains. "It was detrimental to my health and Tucker's. My monthly still came, so I didn't know I was pregnant until I was pretty far along. Knowing that I could've hurt both of us quite badly. If there is any chance that you're ever pregnant, I need you to tell me. I'll buy the test."

"Monthly?" I ask, tears stopping as confusion takes over.

Her eyes widen slightly. "You don't...?"

"Don't what?"

"Bleed every month? Your period—you don't have it?"

I stare at her, a tissue still clenched in my hand. "Cecilia, what are you talking about?"

"Is there any chance you're pregnant?"

"No."

"Are you sure?"

"I've never even kissed him."

She sighs. "Okay. I will schedule an appointment in the hospital for you when you return. I'm sure you're fine, don't worry. It'll just be a visit with the nutritionist to make sure you're getting enough calories."

"Okay," I say, nodding slowly. "Have you had this conversation with Ava yet?"

She nods as well. "About a month ago, I came by in the evening. You were out, I think."

"Oh. Okay. Do you need anything else from me?"

"No, you're all set. Thank you, Davis. I'll see you tomorrow in the classroom."

"See you then." I rise and grab the box of tissues, placing it back in the supply closet on my way out the door. Once it shuts behind me, I sigh and frown. "What the hell is a monthly?" I mutter, starting the long trek back to my room.

CHAPTER SEVENTEEN

TIME FLIES UNTIL FAREWELL NIGHT, after which it seems to stop completely. The squads who are headed to the Surface gather in the dining hall for a small get-together with exceptional food and fancy dresses. It's not exactly my scene, but it's expected of everyone to attend. Plus, there's dessert.

We dress up fancy again; Sam and Amy wear different dresses, but Ava and I don't have enough credits saved up, so we wear the ones from the Spring Festival. There's more alcohol, which Sam and I steer abundantly clear of this time, and different foods we've never seen before.

"So, what am I looking at?" Ava asks, gingerly holding her bite-sized appetizer in one hand.

"It's called sushi," Amy explains. "It's rice, seaweed, and fish. It's good; you'll like it."

"Seaweed?" Noah asks. "Like, from the ocean?"

"Well, no," she says. "From the labs in 7. But it's grown to be exactly like the real stuff. Trust me, it's good."

"Okay," Ava says doubtfully. "Do I just put the whole thing in my mouth?"

"Yeah, that's the best way to do it," Sam chimes in. "Just eat it, c'mon."

Ava takes a deep breath, laughing a little, then pops the sushi into her mouth. She looks confused for a moment, then slightly repulsed, then content. We all watch with bated breath, waiting for her opinion.

"It's good," she says after swallowing. "Weird at first, but good. Do they have more?"

While Ava and Noah try all the different kinds of sushi, Chris and I wander off. We each order exactly one shot of vodka, which I like a lot less than the whiskey from last time. Regardless, the warmth spreads from my stomach to my fingertips, making me a bit braver.

"Ashborrow, Davis," Cecilia says, coming to stand next to us at the bar. She's dressed up, too, in a purple gown that rolls off her muscular shoulders. 'Boulder shoulders,' Sam called them.

"Cecilia," Chris says, nodding to her. "How are you?"

"Doing pretty well, considering they have mac 'n cheese bites," she says. I think it's the first time I've ever heard her joke. "How are you two doing?"

"We're good, ma'am," I say.

She raises an eyebrow at me. "Davis, what did I say about 'ma'am?'"

"Right, sorry. We're good. Ava and Noah are trying sushi."

"Ah, Omenstat's favorite," Cecilia says, pausing to order a martini. "Never been fond of it, myself, but I'm also pretty picky."

Then, I notice how her handbag, gold and studded with sparkles, is bulging out at the sides. "Cecilia, if I may, what's in there?"

She grins (it might be the first time I've ever seen her do that, too) and pops it open. Inside is about a dozen mac 'n cheese bites, wrapped individually in white napkins.

"Tucker's favorite," she explains, snapping it shut once we get a peek. "He's not feeling well at the moment, so I'm smuggling some out for him. Don't tell anyone."

"Cross my heart," Chris laughs, drawing an 'x' over his chest. "Is he alright?"

"Yes, thank you." Cecilia receives her martini from the bartender, taking a slow sip. "Mm, that's nice. But yes, Tucker's gonna be fine." She says it with the vindication that only mothers with chronically sick children do, but neither of us asks.

"Davis, I have you scheduled for an appointment next week," she continues.

"Oh, thank you."

"And Ashborrow, we're going to chat about getting the rest of your squad down in the hospital with you when you get back. They have a lot to learn, could be valuable."

"Sounds great," Chris replies. "Will we see you in the morning?"

"I'll be there to see you off," Cecilia says, scooping up her glass. "If you'll excuse me, I think I see an old friend by the chocolate fountain. Get some rest tonight."

She ambles away before we can say goodbye, and we turn to look at one another.

"Appointment?" Chris asks.

"With a nutritionist. To make sure I'm eating enough," I explain.

"Oh, gotcha." If he wants to ask, he doesn't say so. Instead, he takes my hand and leads me onto the dance floor as another slow song begins to play.

AVA AND NOAH stay down in the dining hall to get a special dessert for the four of us at the end of the night. The perks of facing potential death, right? Chris and I, tired of being social, retire to our rooms. We part ways to pack our stuff and change, but he enters my room not much later.

"What's in the bag?" I ask as I zip up my backpack. Most of my meager belongings are packed in there, including a note Lucas wrote me for our thirteenth birthdate celebration. I want a piece of him with me should the worst happen.

"Look," Chris says, pulling a canister of spray paint out of the plastic bag he's holding. "I got it at one of the art stores yesterday. Only four credits."

"And what are you planning to do with this red spray paint from one of the art stores?"

"Paint our names on the walls," he says. "You always wanted to leave a mark on the world, right?"

I pause for a moment, slightly taken aback. "Well, alright then," I finally say.

He nods with a glint in his eyes and a contagious smile on his face. We pull one of the beds away from the wall as quietly as possible and shake up the can of spray paint.

"You first," Chris offers.

"Okay." I smile, stealing a deep breath of clean air before uncapping the bottle. The stench is foul and acidic, but the result will be worth it.

I shake the spray paint one last time to ensure that it works, then begin.

The first letter of my name surprises me. The crimson red is a shocking contrast to the creamy beige, and some extra paint drips down the wall. I hurriedly paint the rest of my name, then pass the can to Chris. He scrawls his name right next to mine, so close that the 'e' of mine and the 'c' of his are nearly touching.

"It looks like our names are bleeding," I say quietly.

"Yeah, it does," Chris replies. "Kinda symbolic, I guess."

A grim laugh escapes my lips. "It kinda is."

I think of telling him about my conversation with Cecilia a few days ago—we haven't been alone together since—but hold off. There's no sense in making him self-conscious about us, about whatever's going on here and the fact that she can see it, too. If I tell him someone else can see, it makes it real. I'm not sure I'm ready for that.

We sit in silence, the ticking of the wall clock the only sound in this quiet world. Our names slowly dry along with the dripping crimson. Within minutes our names are permanent. We will stay here forever, no matter what happens tomorrow.

We're staring at each other, and I realize what's going to happen only a moment before it does; we're nose-to-nose, and he's looking at my mouth. And finally, I get my fairytale moment, even better than I had imagined. It only lasts for a few seconds, but it is good, and it is right because he is. Chris is good, and he is right.

In silence, we sit with our foreheads pressed together, breathing even and deep. Hearts racing and minds sharp, we each wait for the other to lean back in.

The door slams open suddenly; Ava and Noah briskly walk in. Chris and I leap to our feet with reddened cheeks, and the force of our movement pushes the bed against the wall, hiding our crime scene.

"They were out of lemon meringue!" Ava cries. "*OUT!* I had to settle for red velvet cake, but at least it has the cream cheese frosting. Katie, we got you pecan pie, and Chris, you got peach. Noah got some kind of peanut-butter-chocolate ball of death."

"Chocolate peanut butter bomb!" Noah says, setting down his tray. Maybe later, there'll be an explosive rock in his gut; we don't usually get to eat such unhealthy food. A soldier's diet may enhance performance, but it sucks when you crave chocolate and get chicken breast with roasted vegetables. Then again, Cecilia did say something about me potentially needing more calories. Maybe there's more dessert in my future.

"Here you go," Noah says, handing me my pie and a plastic fork.

"Thanks." I force my voice to be calm. Chris echoes me, and we all eat in silence, savoring our desserts. I steal a bite of everyone else's, and they all steal a bite of mine.

My mother would make pies when pecans were on sale at the store. This pie is good, but hers was better.

We just sit when we finish, quiet and calm. Ava and Noah still wear their dress clothes. I don't say anything about the spray paint, which is selfish, but I don't want to share that moment. I want us to be the only people to ever know about those two bloody words. By the time someone paints over them, we will be long gone. We could be gone by tomorrow night.

"We should all stay in here," Noah says, breaking the silence. "One last time. Sleepover?"

"Yeah," Chris says, glancing at me. "Let's go get our stuff."

Chris and Noah leave, bringing the remnants of dessert with them.

I don't want Ava to die never knowing about what just happened. "Chris kissed me while you guys were gone."

She puts on a fresh pair of leggings, looking completely unfazed, which contrasts my overactive mind. "Took you two long enough. Noah and I first kissed, like, a month ago."

"Yeah, but we were all expecting that, and it's… I don't know. It's not a big deal for you two."

"Wanna know why it wasn't a big deal?" she asks. I nod. "We just didn't make it one. Relax—savor the moment. You happy?"

"Very."

"He a good kisser?"

"Very."

"Then that's all that you need. Just take it as it comes."

The boys return some minutes later carrying travel backpacks and wearing sweats. They will not be returning to their room in the morning, or maybe ever.

"Why do I have a feeling that none of us is going to get any sleep?" Noah asks, dropping his backpack by the door and kicking off his sneakers.

Ava spits her mouthwash into the sink, passing me the bottle. "Because we won't be."

"Nerves?" Chris sits down on the edge of my bed.

"Nope. You realize it makes more sense for us to stay up than it does for us to sleep for only a few hours and try to wake up?"

"Ugh, you're right," I say. "I'll stay up with you. What time is it?"

She looks at the clock. "9:03."

"Ugh."

"Anyone wanna play a game?" Noah asks. "There's one called Would You Rather, where you give someone two options, and they pick the one they would rather do."

"Sure, I'll play," I say, sitting down next to Chris. "Noah, tell me. Would you rather eat live spiders or earthworms?"

Ava throws a pillow at me. "Gross!"

"Yeah." Noah wrinkles his nose, trying to avoid giving an answer.

"Noah Evan Grim," I say, narrowing my eyes jokingly. "Answer. Me."

"Earthworms!" He throws his hands up in surrender. "Spiders would be crunchy, and they move too much."

"Didn't need reasoning," Chris says, grimacing. "Totally unnecessary."

"Your turn," I say to Chris.

He thinks for a moment before asking me, "Would you rather lick an electrical socket or a doorknob?"

"Doorknob. I'm not electrocuting my tongue. Hell no."

We spend the entire night like that, trying to ignore the fact that we may never do this again. Chris takes my hand at some point, and eventually, I end up leaning against him. Ava and Noah fall asleep before we do, tucked into each other and holding on like it's the end of the world.

Once they're asleep, Chris and I shut off the lights and lay back down on my bed. He falls asleep with his head on my chest. The green light of the smoke detector stares down at me while I think.

I once told my mother that the phrase "life is short" was stupid. At six years old, I thought that phrase made no sense because I knew life was the longest thing any of us would ever experience. Now I understand. Each day is long, sometimes even infinite, yet at the end of it, all I know is that it was too short. I want more; I deserve more, but I might not get it. I don't know if I did something wrong; if perhaps I angered some almighty power that decided I wasn't good enough. Will I ever be good enough? Will any of us be?

I remember my mother teaching me what to do in moments like this. When her head was fuzzy, she would make lists. In this moment I know very little, so I make a list of the few things I *do* know.

One: I am still alive. My heart is beating, my lungs are breathing, and my stomach is digesting that slice of pecan pie. I am still alive.

Two: I care too much about my squad to let them die. They need to live even if I don't. They deserve this chance.

Three: I feel something for Chris that I've never felt for anyone else. I can't explain it, but I know because... I just do.

Four: Sometimes logic and reasoning can't answer your questions; sometimes, you just have to feel it. Sometimes that's the only way you ever know anything. Sometimes you just do.

CHAPTER EIGHTEEN

Cecilia is the first thing I see that morning. Her face hovers just above mine, and I practically leap out of my skin.

"Ankou, Cecilia," I say, shoving Chris off of me. "How... why?"

"I forgot to give you an alarm clock last night," she replies, looking from Chris to me and then back to Chris. "Sleep well?" Her voice has a hint of teasing in it, despite the situation.

"Sure, yeah," I reply. Ava is already brushing her teeth, and Noah is standing in the middle of the room with a dumbfounded expression. I briefly wonder if he's sleepwalking until he speaks.

"What time is it?" he asks, voice hoarse.

"1:30," Cecilia says, checking her watch. "I want all of you in the bay in 30 minutes max. You have a long day ahead—you can rest on the ride."

She leaves briskly, making sure to close the door softly so as not to wake our neighbors. I realize I never met the kids living in this hall with us. We need to do that when we get home—if we get home.

"We got two hours of sleep," Chris says as he trades place with Ava, splashing his face with cold water. "Who the hell thought that was a good idea?"

"Not me," Noah says, with a pointed look at Ava as she yawns.

"If our mission isn't until late tonight, why are we leaving so early?" I ask, not really expecting an answer.

Chris, always informed, gives me one anyway. "We have to get to base camp with a lot of time to spare, and it's safer to ship us out in the middle of the night. It's a six-hour ride; we can sleep on the way. Once we get there, we have to be fully functioning to assist in medical tents and prepare."

"Anyone remember what time we leave?" Ava asks. Chris, once again, has the answer.

"2:30."

We work in silence, brushing our teeth and getting changed. I throw my bullet-proof shirt over my sports bra and change into my tights, annoyed by just how skin-tight they really are. I may as well be naked; you can see the muscles in my legs.

I throw some gel in my hair to keep it from falling in my eyes, brush my teeth, and wash my face. I am all too aware that it could be my last time doing any of this but try to force the thought away.

"Ready?" Chris says when I step back out of the bathroom. Everyone is lacing up their boots, and I hurry to join them.

"Ready," I say, forcing confidence into my voice. I am sure; I am prepared; I am ready. I can do this.

"It is a six-hour ride to base camp," Cecilia says, voice quiet. She sits on one of the dining tables, sipping coffee while the six of us stand around her in a semicircle. "Once there, you might get a room or tent if you're lucky. If not, you'll stay in the common area or help in the field hospital. I would advise you to help out wherever necessary if you do not get a room. Keep your mind busy, but do not physically strain yourself. You'll need your energy."

"Any other advice?" Sam asks. Her exterior is confident, arms crossed with a determined look in her eyes. I can only imagine the panic she must feel inside, knowing what happened the last time she went to the Surface for a mission of this caliber.

"Try not to die," Cecilia says as she hops off the table. I have a feeling that this conversation has happened before between the three of them.

"Thank you, Cecilia," Ava says, re-adjusting her bag on her shoulder. "For everything."

Cecilia holds up her hand. "Thank me when you get back."

"Of course," Ava replies and begins to say something else before the Head Trainer cuts her off.

"Squads 5607, 5608, 5609, and 5610, please report unaccompanied to the front of the dining hall!"

People begin saying their final goodbyes, giving last hugs, and walking away from their families.

Cecilia nods confidently. "Make me look good up there."

I nod with the weight of unshed tears behind my eyes—despite my best efforts, fear is seeping into my blood. I don't want to let her down; she's the closest thing I have to a parent now that mine are both gone. I don't want to have to say goodbye to her, too.

Pushing it all away as best I can, I follow Sam and Amy to the front of the room. On the way, I see a girl holding onto her boyfriend, not wanting to let go.

He is quietly reassuring her— "Babe, hey, I'll see you when I get home. It's okay."

The sight makes my chest ache nearly as much as walking away from Cecilia did.

"Soldiers," the Head Trainer begins once all the squads stand in a group. In total, there can be no more than thirty of us. The boy now stands alone; his girlfriend is in the dining hall doorway, hovering for one more moment before exiting by herself.

"Comrades, friends. Family. Over these years, you have forged unshakeable bonds that have stood the test of time and will continue to do so until the end. What you are about to do is daunting, yes, but I have chosen you for a reason. You are strong, dependable, and courageous people in whom I have put the utmost faith. Make me proud up there."

All of us salute him. He salutes us in return before directing us to the same rocky tunnel we walked down last time.

"Sam!" someone calls. Antoinette Latrodectus jogs to catch up to us. "Can I talk to you guys? Actually, everyone."

"Oh, um, sure," Sam says, making room for Antoinette to walk into our group.

"I'm so sorry for all these years that I—"

"It's done," Sam says firmly, reassuring her. "It's over now, Antoinette. Don't apologize; make up for the past with the future."

Antoinette nods shakily as the light grows in front of us. We arrive in the bay, and she says nothing more before climbing into the first car.

"What was that?" I ask once she's gone. "I thought you guys hated each other."

Sam answers with a bite in her voice that wasn't there before. "That was a soldier trying to apologize for the past because she wants to die with a clear conscience."

"Sam," Amy hisses, but says nothing more.

We find Earl's car and clamber inside, saying quick hellos and getting settled as fast as we can. We've in a van this time, one with a top, so we move with hunched backs as we clamber into the bench seats. They face forward, so we are all looking through the windshield. I glance at the clock on the dashboard; 2:29.

Earl sticks a thumb out the window, and I peer around Sam to notice the other drivers doing the same. I take Chris's hand as the engine comes alive.

I feel Chris squeeze my hand tightly, and I squeeze back. "You okay?" I keep my voice low, so only he can hear me.

"Yes." He pushes the word through his teeth.

After about a minute or so, the engine dies down, and the car starts to move. We roll out slowly, the motion bumpy. Chris's death grip gradually weakens to a more tolerable one, prompting less panicked thoughts of how I will tie up guards with one hand.

The car picks up speed, and the loading station is quickly left behind. All around us are whoops and hollers as other soldiers stick their arms, or even their heads, out of the windows. Sam opens the one next to her, sticking her hand out. The wind rips my hair from its gel cast, but I don't mind. I have another tube in my bag.

The tunnel begins to lighten, and the soldiers in front of us retreat into their cars, pulling the windows closed after them. Sam double checks the lock on the now-closed window. Earl sits up a bit straighter, slowing the car to match the pace of those in front of us. This part, this nearing of the exit, is the worst.

After another minute of unyielding tension, we emerge into the moonlight. My hopes are realized—the sky is clear! The grass is tall enough to touch if Sam would only open the window and stick her hand out, and the stars look so close I could grab them from their inky tapestry. They've changed slightly since we last saw them, but the constellations are familiar. The air smells like rain; we just missed a storm. We press tire marks into the damp grass, leaving the tunnel behind. All around us, the cars fan out, moving in an obvious forma-tion to spread the tracks apart.

Sam, Amy, and Earl relax into their seats, the tension falling from their shoulders.

"We're in the clear now," Early says. "Music?"

"Classic rock?" Sam requests.

"You got it." Earl presses a button on the console, and music pours out, electric guitar and drums and a man screaming his lungs out.

"Thanks, Earl!" Amy shouts, closing her eyes and tipping her head back to absorb the music. I also close my eyes, feeling the bass pulse in my stomach. Someone cracks a window, and the wind catches the back of my neck. Goosebumps erupt across my shoulders, partially from the cold and partially from the song. I, somehow, fall asleep to the sound of classic rock, the engine humming, and Noah and Sam talking about pollen.

I forgot he has allergies.

CHAPTER NINETEEN

GETTING across the plains takes us through the sunrise, and then we drive through the woods on a dirt road until late morning. Chris falls asleep with his head in my lap for an hour, but I wake him when we reach a cleared part of the forest. Suddenly I am no longer fearless.

"We made it," Earl says as he parks the car and reclines his seat. "You guys head on over to the tents and get yourselves registered. I'm takin' a nap."

"Thanks, Earl," Sam says as she climbs down, followed by a chorus of thank yous.

Chris jumps down before me and extends a hand that I take even though I don't need to. The forest smells of sap and sunlight. The grass is feathery and soft underfoot, pine trees creaking in the light breeze.

"Welcome to camp," a girl says. She has flaming red hair and freckles splashed across her whole face like her parents asked for polka dots. A clipboard rests on her hip, and a stethoscope hangs from her neck. "Registration tent's back behind the med tents."

"Thanks," Amy says, leading us through the small maze of tents and bustling medics. There are dirt roads between them, some worn by footsteps and some by tire treads.

"It's quiet," Sam comments.

"We got here quick," Amy says.

"You call this quiet?" I ask Sam.

"Yep."

We file into the registration tent, which is smaller than the others. A white folding table is set up in the middle with an older man and woman standing behind it.

"Hello," the woman says kindly. "What can I do for ya?"

"Squad 5609, here for tonight's mission." Amy holds up her badge. We all do the same, and the man makes six check marks on a piece of paper.

"Alright." The woman smiles. "Food tents are out that'a way—" she points north. "And ya saw the med tents. A car'll pick ya up 'round seven and bring ya to the air pad. Best'a luck to ya."

"Thank you," we chorus, saluting them and exiting the tent.

"Anybody hungry?" Sam asks.

"I could eat," Noah says, glancing down and patting his stomach.

"You could *always* eat," Chris jokes, rolling his eyes. The gesture, accompanied by a rare smile, makes him look like he did when we were just kids. The sunlight looks good on his face. "Anyone else?"

"I'm down for food," I say.

Ava nods. "Same."

We make our way to the food tents, where many other soldiers our age are milling around. My feet itch to be let out of my boots and walk on the cool grass, but that would be weird. I wonder if Meliors have ever felt grass underfoot and realize then that I would take being an Avenda any day. I was so lucky to live here.

We grab food from the buffet-style setup and find seats a short distance away from the rest of the squads.

"Anyone have the time?" a short boy asks, approaching us. His caramel-colored afro falls in his eyes as he jogs. "I'm leaving at noon."

Ava checks her watch. "11:45. When's your report time?"

"Five minutes ago!" he shouts, turning and sprinting towards the cars. "Thanks!"

"They're sending people in now?" I ask, taking a bite of my hamburger. "Why so early?"

"Scouts," Amy replies. She takes a sip of water before continuing, "Gotta take a people estimate, see how it'll be later on tonight."

"They've got the hardest jobs in the whole army," Sam mutters. "Going into the city like civilians, all radioed and wired. Poor bastards."

"As civilians?" Noah asks. "Why?"

"We can't just storm in there without knowing where we're going," Chris says.

"But isn't there a Border?" Ava asks. "How can civilians just come and go?"

"They'll hop on the back of the train," Amy explains. "And hop back off when it passes through the Border. Tech squads will disable the cameras as they go by. They'll walk the streets for a little while—it's a big enough city that there shouldn't be anyone who realizes they don't belong there. They'll radio back after a few hours, then an aerial team will pick them up and bring them back as we go in."

"Oh. That sounds rough."

"Yeah, I don't envy them."

"Wait, won't they know we're coming if the cameras go down?" I ask.

Sam waves the crust of her sandwich at me. "We have to keep the window small, and we've been messing with them for a few weeks now. They think the system just keeps malfunctioning. That was our mistake with Carcera. We took the cameras down hours in advance and hadn't done anything to them before, so they knew something was up. Window is way smaller today."

"Oh, okay."

"Wait, so what is this place?" Noah asks, glancing around at the rusty remnants of old picnic tables and water pumps that seem to be as much a part of the landscape as the trees.

"An old campground, I think. Like, for fun."

We all stare at her.

"For camping?" She tries. "Oh, Jesus Christ. People used to come here to sleep, way before Borders."

"Because they were on the run?" Ava asks.

"No, for fun. They'd bring a tent or an RV, which is like a big car with a living space in it. They'd sleep out here, enjoy the scenery, stuff like that."

"For fun?" Chris clarifies.

"Yes. God, do you people have a lot to learn."

Our lack of knowledge makes me feel less confident about tonight —what if there's information that we need to know that we simply don't? What else has fallen through the cracks in classroom studies?

We head to the medical tent after lunch, at least Chris and I do. Sam and Amy wander off to explore the woods and relax, and Ava and Noah offer their assistance in the food tent.

As we step inside, Chris's eyes light up in a way they probably shouldn't. There aren't too many injured, primarily sprains and scrapes, but it's his area of expertise.

"I need some gauze!" a medic says, pressing on the hand of a young man. He moans in pain as Chris hurries to grab some. I grab a roll of tape.

"Thanks," the medic says, hurriedly pouring some water over the wound and doing a double take. "You're not a medic."

"No, sir," Chris says. "Squad 5609, here to help."

"You stay right there till I'm done," the medic says to me, then turns to Chris. "You, hand me bandages when I say so. This GSW's pretty nasty."

"What happened?" Chris asks.

"Cleaning and prepping rifles for tonight. Didn't know one was loaded."

We work silently for a few minutes until the medic nods and wipes his sweaty forehead.

"All clean. Can you two go and get me some morphine from the supply tent? It's in the green bin, prepackaged and labeled."

"Hell yeah, morphine," the man says, his first words that aren't swears.

"On it," Chris says, and I step out with him. We walk to the supply tent, the backs of our hands bumping together. Neither of us moves apart.

"So," I say once we're in the tent, searching the foldable shelves for morphine. "Last night..."

"Yeah," he says.

Neither of us talks for a moment, and I glance at him with raised eyebrows. He busies himself with scanning the shelves while pretending not to notice my stare.

"Does it mean...?" I ask, unable to finish my sentence.

"Yeah." He says it with such finality—I wish I were that sure.

"Right." I nod, the uncertainty obvious in my voice. "Yeah."

He glances over at me with one eyebrow raised. "You okay?"

I nod again and swallow thickly. Why does he make me so nervous all of a sudden? It's a good feeling but disorienting, nonetheless. "I'm fine."

"Okay," he replies, pulling a vial of morphine off the shelf. "Let's go."

We collide on our way out of the supply tent, and my lips end up dangerously close to his. I look up at him as he leans down, trying to seal the gap between us—

And someone throws open the tent flap. Chris and I don't jump away from each other this time; there's not enough room for that. Instead, we snap our heads towards the person so fast I hear his neck crack. He removes his hands from my waist, and I pull mine from his chest.

"Called it!" Noah shouts, fist-pumping the air. "Yes!"

"Noah, calm down," Chris hisses. "Be quiet."

"Oh, yeah," Noah says sheepishly. A smug grin replaces his ecstatic expression. He crosses his arms across his chest. "So, how long has this been going on? Did I ruin your moment? Sorry, didn't mean to ruin your first—"

"This isn't our first kiss," I say.

Noah's jaw drops. "What? Dude, why did nobody tell me?"

"It was *yesterday!*" Chris says. "C'mon, a guy with a shot hand needs some morphine."

"If he could wait for you to suck face, he can wait for you to explain *why* you were sucking face."

"For your information," I say, snatching the morphine out of Chris's hand and ducking under Noah's arm. "He does not *suck face.*"

"Uh-huh, sure." Noah smiles.

I roll my eyes, and Chris shoves his arm lightly as we return to the med tent, linking his elbow in mine.

"What was that?" I whisper, a giddy smile spreading across my cheeks like a wildfire over dead brush.

"Failed attempt number 183." Chris giggles. It's a beautiful change to hear his voice so light.

"You've tried to kiss me 182 other times?" I ask, raising one eyebrow.

"Why wouldn't I?" he replies, glancing over at me with a grin on his face.

I kiss his cheek lightly as we step back into the med tent, suddenly braver.

HOURS LATER, when the night is just starting to descend upon the valley, we get the call.

"Katie!" Ava shouts up at me. I'm at the top of a tree by myself, taking in the landscape. Mountains surround the camp, some of them capped by snow. Rivers poke their way down their sides; the sun disappeared into the west not ten minutes ago. I can't help but feel homesick. That wasn't enough sunlight for me, but the red and gold streaks still painted across the sky will have to do.

"Is it time?" I ask

She nods once, and I sigh, glancing out at the horizon again. Slowly I begin my descent, carefully picking my way through this oak's twisted limbs. I jump the last ten feet and shake the impact out of my ankles.

"You ready?" she asks.

"I just have to grab my helmet," I reply, walking with her back to camp. My tree was a short distance away—I call it mine because my initials are freshly carved into one of the topmost branches.

"You ready?" she repeats.

"Are you?" I ask quietly.

"Stop avoiding my question."

"Stop avoiding mine."

All she does is stare at me, and I do the same. Her hair is gathered in a high bun—it has to stay out of her face, but I don't know if it'll fit under her helmet like that. She isn't ready. Am I?

"Let's go," she says quietly.

"C'mere," I say instead, pulling her into a tight hug. "We got this piece of lemon meringue. Right?"

"Right," she says, pulling away. There's the Ava that I know—smiling through it. Two black eyes and a busted lip couldn't keep her down, and they haven't yet.

We make our way to the loading center, where the rest of our squad is already waiting for us.

"Glad to see you all made it," Sam mumbles, and Amy shoots her a glare.

"Can you go over the plan one more time?" Noah asks.

"We go in via helicopter," Sam explains, grabbing a stick and mapping it out in the dirt. "Land on the roof, make our way down the stairwells in the corners—" she draws a line moving down the sides of the building. "Make it to the upper guard's rooms first, then the Head Trainer. Tie him up, tie up the others, then call for the helicopter and get the hell out of there. Other crews will come in to load them into a transport helicopter."

"We have to stay quiet," Amy says. "Get as many as we can before the others know. If people wake up before they're gagged and tied, this whole thing goes to hell."

"What about the helicopter?" Chris asks. "Isn't that going to be loud?"

"New tech," Sam explains. "Instead of blades on top, mini ones in the bottom displace air so that it can pretty much float. It's almost perfectly quiet."

The silence that follows is eerie and hushed, like the rest of the world decided to stop with us. All I can see at that moment is that my friends, my *best* friends, are no longer kids. We've grown up in a way that we would never have if we stayed behind the Border, and in a way that I'm not sure we should've. But no matter where we spent the last three months, we would've grown up too fast.

"5609!" Earl shouts, leaning out of the window of his car. "You ready?"

"All set," Amy replies, pulling herself up into the car and extending a hand to the rest of us. I grab a helmet from the bin beside the car, shoving it onto my head as I take my seat.

"I'm takin' ya a few miles south of here," Earl says. His goggles give his eyes a yellowish tint. "To the air pad. The building has already been infiltrated by a tech squad—they took down radar and cameras —but they're out of there, so don't worry about them. Got it?"

"Yes, sir," Sam says, sitting beside Amy and taking her hand. Ava sits in front of me, and I end up sandwiched between Noah and Chris. The ride is silent as dusk falls, then night.

Earl gets us herded into the helicopter, and we quickly say goodbye to him. Sam and Amy hug him while the rest of us salute him.

Inside the helicopter, things are cramped. My knees bump against Chris's, who sits across from me this time. We take off within ten minutes, and all I do is stare at the floor between our feet.

When I glance out the window, my stomach drops. We rush past the forest and weave between mountains, and the sight of the earth so far away makes me sick. I don't care that we may never do this again —I want to be back on the ground.

The ride takes almost an hour, and soon the Border is looming. It's smaller than Carcera's—at least, it looks that way from way up here— but the sight still sends me into a spiral. I can't be back in there, can't be inside the walls again.

We soon plop down softly on the roof of the Army Center, and I find my breath again as I focus on the task at hand. Sam exits first and motions for the rest of us to follow her. She puts a finger to her lips.

We hop down from the helicopter, the flat stone hard on my ankles. I glance around at my friends, signing the words, *Everybody ready?*

I get a variety of *yes's* and give the thumbs up to the pilot. He salutes us, taking off into the night again. We are left in silence, with no wind, no birdsong. This is the tallest building in the city, and it feels like we've come to the top of the world.

Let's get off the roof, Sam signs. *Too obvious.*

Low wall Noah signs. He points to an enclosed area with a small wall around it.

Chris shakes his head, signing the words, *Garden. No footprints.*

Let's just start Ava signs. Her eyes are colder than I've ever seen them. *Noah, you go west.* She points to Chris and me, then Sam and Amy. *Stay in pairs. Cover everything.*

I tap Noah's radio to remind them that we have it. Everyone nods, and we disperse.

Chris and I head to the north stairwell with knives already drawn, coils of rope draped around our necks, and towels thrown over our shoulders. Amy and Sam move to the south, Noah goes to the west, and Ava has already disappeared down the eastern stairwell.

"Fool," I whisper, shaking my head as we reach the door.

"She'll be fine," Chris replies, opening the door and wincing as the hinges squeak. He holds it open for me. "After you."

"Thanks," I whisper. "You cover back; I cover front."

We catch each other's gaze for a moment as the door closes behind us. A shaft of moonlight falls over his eyes, turning them blue-gray. For a moment, I think he might kiss me, and I hope he will, but then he stops short. I hadn't even noticed how we leaned toward each other until we pull apart.

"You ready?" he whispers, eyes darting everywhere but my face.

"Are you?" I ask.

A soft smile breaks onto his face as he finally looks back at me. "I got your back."

I can't help but smile for a moment, then turn around and begin to pad down the stairwell, footsteps hushed against the stone. The descent feels both endless and shockingly quick as we reach a door that reads GUARD DORMITORIES.

"Ready?" Chris whispers. His voice sounds so loud that it's a wonder the guards don't wake up immediately.

I nod—it's much darker down here. I glance up the stairwell and can make out the edge of the nearly-full moon.

"We'll see it again," Chris murmurs, reading my thoughts.

"Damn right," I reply. We slip through the door, closing it softly behind us and locking it. No one can escape unless they pay enough attention to unlock it, including us.

Inside is a narrow hallway with doors down one side, dimly lit by LED lamps hanging on the walls. The sound of my breath is ringing in my ears, and the rate of it feels hard to control.

I point to the end of the hallway, where a silhouette is visible. Chris presses me against the wall with one arm even though I'm already stepping back.

Neither of us dares to breathe as we watch the figure step out of one of the rooms, hearts pounding in our chests. The figure carefully closes the door behind them, staying near the wall as they approach another one. As the figure passes under a light, I recognize its face as Ava's.

She's already halfway done, I sign.

Chris shakes his head. *She needs to be more careful.*

After she gracefully disappears inside the next room, we finally move.

I'll tie them. You don't have to he signs.

Yes, I do. As we step up to the door, I press a finger to my lips. The metal handle taunts me as I take a deep breath, then another. Chris puts a hand on the small of my back, sending electric sparks up my spine. Finally, I put a hand on the cool metal and twist it. The door doesn't even squeak as it swings open to reveal the two sleeping men inside. They are so used to being safe that they didn't bother to lock it.

One of them snores so loudly that I jump, but we enter the room anyway. Our footsteps are light, nearly silent as we approach the beds. My eyes lock with Chris's as I pull out a towel, fingers trembling so much I fear it will slip out of my palm.

He nods, somehow telling me everything he needs to say without speaking a word. He tells me that it's okay, that it's not real, that I can do this. He tells me everything Cecilia would do but with his blue eyes, and it means so much more for them.

I remember how we laughed when we learned to do this, remember the heartbeats in my stomach and the way Ava winked at me when I got home that night. Remember how he looked from above, and from below. Remember committing it to memory.

I look down at the snoring man again. It's so easy to wish them death when they wear their masks. His hair is auburn brown, the same color as mine, and he looks no older than I. For a moment, I think it's Lucas, but my mind proves my heart wrong—Lucas doesn't have a birthmark under his left eye. The man asleep before me is taller than Lucas ever was, more muscular and filled out than he ever got to be. It isn't him, of course, because my brother is dead.

This man could've been the one to kill him and my parents, for all I know. This man could've shot Natasha and Levi; he could've arrested Victor Castellano and thrown him in jail to rot. This man could've murdered people, real, living people who I loved.

I stuff the gag into his mouth.

CHAPTER TWENTY

As I GAG the sleeping soldier, I leap onto the bed with as much grace and poise as I can muster, straddling him as I tie his hands behind his back. Chris struggles with his guard for not much longer than I do. Soon both men are staring at us in terror, waiting for us to kill them. Part of me wants to see the blood on my hands, just to see what revenge would feel like. But then I remember that killing them won't bring my family back, and I leave them be.

WE GO through the next four rooms without a problem. Eventually, we meet up with Sam, Amy, and Noah.

"Where's Ava?" Noah whispers.

"Right here," Ava whispers, stepping out of the shadows. She's covered in blood, crimson splattered across her face and dripping from her hands. Our eyes go wide as she joins our small circle tucked into the crevice of a stairwell, and we all unconsciously recoil.

"What happened?" Noah whispers, eyes bulging from his head. The blood all over her is still wet; she's practically leaving a puddle on the floor.

He woke up and grabbed a knife Ava signs. *This is his.*

We all know she's in shock, but we have no time to take care of her. She'll be fine once we get out of here.

"The Head Trainer is on the next floor," Sam whispers. "Only two should go. Everyone else should start bringing soldiers to the roof and getting them ready for the assisting squads. Amy?"

"I'll go with you," she murmurs.

Sam smiles at her. "Alright. You four start bringing them to the roof, help the evac. The team gets them on the helicopter when they get here. Do not wait for us. We'll either meet you or—"

"We'll see you on the roof," Noah says quietly, reaching out momentarily as if to pull Sam into a hug. She stiffens and raises her eyebrows, a look of 'keep it together, we're professionals.'

Noah pulls up short, letting the two of them walk into the shadows. A pit grows in my stomach, and I have only a moment to sense the impending doom before it arrives.

The soldier materializes behind Noah with his knife drawn.

Ava wordlessly shoves him away, taking the blow instead. The knife is plunged into her lower back to the right of her spine, and while her bulletproof shirt saves her from a death blow, it's still deep.

She arches away from the pain, silently falling to her knees. Chris has a knife in the soldier's throat before I can reach him, but someone's already picking me up from behind. I scream and elbow them in the stomach, dropping all my weight to the floor and putting a foot in their crotch. They pull away, and I slash with my knife as I turn. The motion opens a shallow gash on the man's chest, but it isn't enough to bring him down.

I stab at him and somehow move fast enough to put a foot between his ribs, sending him to the floor. I drop to my knees beside him and plunge the knife into his heart. The struggle is over within seconds, and oh my God, I just killed someone.

"They found us," Chris pants, helping me to my feet. Two dead soldiers are next to him, the one who stabbed Ava and another. "Noah, radio in."

Noah calls it in as I kneel beside Ava, hands shaking furiously as I try to figure out what to do. "Ava? Oh God, *Ava*."

Noah continues talking to whoever is on the other side of the radio, eyes wide as two tiny moons as he stares at Ava. "Whole squad is alive. Two injuries. I need a time frame *now*." He wipes some blood away from the gash on his jaw, but it pours immediately down his neck again. Chris pulls a towel out of his bag and offers it to Noah while pressing another against Ava's back. She groans as he twists to reach behind him for another one. Her blood is soaking his hands, and the smell makes my knees shake.

Some more static, and Noah sighs. "No, for fuck's sake! Come get us. There's a soldier—" His voice tightens. "—bleeding out as we speak." He presses the 'mute' button. "Katie, go get Sam and Amy."

"On it," I say, standing on shaky legs.

Before anyone can stop me, I jog off into the darkness. As I reach the stairwell, I look back one last time. Noah swings Ava into his arms; she's barely conscious. Chris glances over at me, nodding to let me know it's okay. I nod back as I push open the door and begin my descent, tearing my eyes away as they enter the other stairwell.

This stairwell is darker than the other. My footsteps echo like drums as I jog down the stairs as quietly as I can, with no time to move in silence.

I make it to the next floor, pushing open the creaking door with my shoulder. My knife is out and ready, eyes darting from shadow to shadow. I half-expect someone to be waiting for me to let my guard down, hiding in every corner. No one is, but I never do.

"Sam?" I whisper, finding my way into the oppressive darkness. I creep along the wall, searching for any sign of my friends. "Amy?"

Sam steps out of a room with wide eyes. *Go back.*

They woke up. I reply, suddenly overwhelmed by the whole situation. I press down the lump in my throat. *Ava stabbed. We must go.*

No Amy signs, standing next to her. *Almost there.*

Backup is coming now. I explain, hands shaking. I breathe deep, trying to steady them as I continue. *We must go, or we're going to die.*

"You think we're going to die?" Sam hisses, her jaw hardening. Her voice sounds impossibly loud in the silence. "You really have that little faith in us?"

"Noah has the radio. If you don't come now, then this could become a suicide mission. Sam, don't make me go without you, please."

"I'm not going anywhere." Sam looks at Amy. "Are you?"

"Not if you're not," Amy answers. She looks back at me. "Tell them we had no choice."

Something's wrong; Amy never *has* to do anything.

They caught you, I sign, and she nods ever so slightly.

Go, she signs.

Not without you.

Sam puts a hand on my arm and leans in close. She murmurs the next word, sending chills through my spine. "Run."

I tear down the corridor before I can stop myself. A whirlwind of chaos opens up around me; doors yanked open in my wake. I have to make it to the stairwell, I have to make it to the roof, I can't stop—

An unearthly weight sends me crashing to the floor, and my head flies back when my helmet connects with it. Someone straddles my back, and they yell for assistance. "I've got one alive!"

The knife is still in my hand; it's a wonder I didn't impale myself. Somehow, I am able to thrust an arm behind me and stab my captor in the thigh. He screams in pain, putting all the weight on his other leg, and I roll out from under him. I jump to my feet and take off running again, but people are on all sides of me. Doors fly open as I run toward the man blocking the stairwell. I throw the knife and hit him in the shoulder, but all he does is flinch and curse. Now all I have is my gun and no time to unhook it from the holster on my hip.

"Katie!" someone yells in a voice too familiar to be here.

No, there's no way—he can't be here. It's impossible, but I know that voice. I would know that voice anywhere. *Lucas.*

"Katie, stop!" he yells. I don't slow down, I don't stop, but I see him at the end of the hallway next to the man with the knife in his shoulder. Arms are reaching out now, grabbing me and pinning me down like one of those butterflies on display, trapped behind the glass. I am forced to the ground, and my head slams off the floor again.

"Don't hurt her!" Lucas yells as someone handcuffs me, grabbing the back of my helmet and slamming my head into the floor. My vision swims as I writhe under the immense weight. I know it's pointless, but I have to try. I have to make it to the stairwell, I have to make it to the roof, I can't stop now.

Lucas fights his way to the front of the crowd even as the pistols are trained on him. Someone shoves him away, but he shoves them back. "That's my sister!"

"Lucas?" I cough, blood from my lip spewing over the cold cement floor.

"Katie!" he shouts as people push him away. Someone kicks me in the side, white-hot pain flaring in my ribs.

I struggle again, bucking my hips to unseat my captor.

"Stop fighting!" Lucas orders. "Katie, you have to stop fighting them."

"No!" I shout, voice raw from the blood in my throat. "Let me go!"

They bang my head into the floor again, and I groan in pain. I have to make it to the stairwell, I have to make it to the roof, I can't stop now.

"Get off me!" I yell, pistol pressing into my hip. If I can reach around and grab it, I can—no. My hands are cuffed behind my back. This is why we tied the soldiers' hands behind their backs.

"Katie, let it go," Lucas says. He's closer now; his voice is quiet. Maybe I'm just hearing him in my head. Is that a thing, twin telepathy? Or is that just a myth? I'd never heard of it before the Underground.

"No!" I have to force the words through gritted teeth as tears pool in my squeezed-shut eyes. "I can't stop fighting. I *need* them!"

"You'll see them again." His voice is so soft. I can only hear him, no one else.

"When?" A tear slips down my cheek as my exhausted body relaxes.

"In due time."

"You're not even here! You died!" I'm trying not to cry, but it's too hard. I miss my brother, and I miss my parents. I miss home. I want to go home.

"Open your eyes."

My eyes fly open as I am yanked to my feet, stumbling to keep my balance without my arms for help. Two soldiers flank me, pushing me towards the stairwell. I could make a break for it and run, but I'd be shot immediately. I can't help but look up to where the moon is still shining down, casting blue light on my face. A blade of the helicopter is just visible—they're still here.

"Go!" I scream, praying they'll hear me through the door. "RUN! Don't wait, GO!"

For a moment, I think I hear Chris yell back, but then they're dragging me down. I think Chris, Ava, and Noah made it to the roof, but where are Sam and Amy? I don't see them; have they been captured, too? Are they even alive? Someone is slapping me to shut me up. When I look toward my assailant, ready to bite the next hand that comes anywhere near my face, I see that it is Lucas. He stops when we make eye contact and shakes his head silently as the guards push me again.

We reach the next landing, and I glance up, hoping to glimpse the night sky just one more time. A sob rises in my throat as I try to pull away, run up the stairs, jump into the helicopter, and fly away from the dark, the pain, and the fear. I want to go home; I want my mother.

I look up again, unsatisfied with my final glimpse of the night sky. If this is the last time I see the stars, I want them to look like they did in the woods, like they will swallow me whole. I want to watch them with Chris's head on my leg, Noah snoring beside me, and Ava mumbling about pirouettes and peanut butter sandwiches in her sleep. My whole body aches to be back in that cave, to smell of smoke and river water.

I watch as the helicopter rises into the sky, silhouetted by the moon. I can't stop, I have to keep going. I have to make it to the roof.

EMMA GRACE

The End

ACKNOWLEDGMENTS

Endless thanks to my parents, Cindy and Dominick, for their tireless support. Without them, this book would never have been written. They've supplied countless hours of listening, a ridiculous plethora of snacks, and an infinite amount of love and support.

To my sister, Rebecca, who sketched my cover art perfectly on the very first try: thank you so much. I owe you a few essays in payment (or half a dozen Starbucks runs).

My grandparents Kathy, Jim, Allan, Luci, Linda, and William (Woody) have always been some of my biggest supporters. From pizza Fridays to letting me ramble on about my stories on the way home from summer camp, they've never stopped being there for me.

To the friends who share names with some of these characters: I promise there is no relation. I (mostly) knew the characters first.

To the friends who *did* inspire these characters: thank you for being some of the best (or worst) people I have ever known. I hope you can see bits of yourselves in these characters whom I have come to love nearly as much as I love you.

Many thanks to Barbara, my first editor, and the first person in the writing industry to take me seriously. I was 14 years old with a smile full of braces, and she treated me like a true professional. Words cannot express my gratitude for that.

A massive thank-you to the entire team at The Paper House, who took me under their wing and helped me to prepare Katie's story for the world to see. They've gone above and beyond to help me prepare my debut novel for publication, fielding frantic emails with grace and ease. They've been a wonderful team to work with, and I couldn't be happier to see my story on the shelves.

And, of course, the largest of thank-you's to all my teachers growing up. Every single one has motivated and encouraged me, from reading my first short stories to asking for signed copies of this book. Extra thanks to Mrs. Jackie DeMenezes, Mrs. Jennifer Hartman Bergen, and Mrs. Carla Chianese Rigolizzo, my elementary school teachers who built the foundation for the writer I am today.